Jayne was perfect for him.

She could match his wit, and give snide comment for snide comment. She could kiss like a dream. Hell, she could even swear. There was only one little problem. She wasn't ready for children.

And Wes Stryker had just petitioned for custody of not one, but two.

Thank goodness he hadn't already fallen in love with her, he told himself. He just had to put her out of his mind.

He'd put women out of his mind before. He could do it again.

By the time he'd pulled his truck between the fence posts lining his driveway, he'd decided it was a good thing he'd discovered this now. A good thing, hell. If it was so good, why did he feel like starting a fight? And why could he still smell the heady scent of her perfume?

Dear Reader,

This April, Silhouette Romance showers you with six spectacular stories from six splendid authors! First, our exciting LOVING THE BOSS miniseries continues as rising star Robin Wells tells the tale of a demure accountant who turns daring to land her boss—and become mommy to *The Executive's Baby*.

Prince Charming's Return signals Myrna Mackenzie's return to Silhouette Romance. In this modern-day fairy-tale romance, wealthy FABULOUS FATHER Gray Alexander discovers he has a son, but the proud mother of his child refuses marriage—unless love enters the equation.... Sandra Steffen's BACHELOR GULCH miniseries is back with *Wes Stryker's Wrangled Wife!* In this spirited story, a pretty stranger just passing through town can't resist a sexy cowboy struggling to raise two orphaned tykes.

Cara Colter revisits the lineup with *Truly Daddy*, an emotional, heartwarming novel about a man who learns what it takes to be a father—and a husband—through the transforming love of a younger woman. When *A Cowboy Comes a Courting* in Christine Scott's contribution to HE'S MY HERO!, the virginal heroine who'd sworn off sexy, stubborn, Stetson-wearing rodeo stars suddenly finds herself falling hopelessly in love. And FAMILY MATTERS showcases Patti Standard's newest novel in which a man with a knack for fixing things sets out to make a struggling single mom and her teenage daughter *His Perfect Family*.

As always, I hope you enjoy this month's offerings, and the wonderful ones still to come!

Happy reading!

Mary-Theresa Hussey

Mary-Theresa Hussey
Senior Editor, Silhouette Romance

Please address questions and book requests to:
Silhouette Reader Service
U.S.: 3010 Walden Ave., P.O. Box 1325, Buffalo, NY 14269
Canadian: P.O. Box 609, Fort Erie, Ont. L2A 5X3

Sandra Steffen

WES STRYKER'S WRANGLED WIFE

Silhouette
R O M A N C E™
Published by Silhouette Books
America's Publisher of Contemporary Romance

For Sally Bulgarelli:

You give great advice. Better yet, you listen (sometimes)
to my great advice. We laugh at the same jokes, cry at
the same injustices and know what's important. Were we
sisters in another lifetime? Maybe. Friends in this one?
Certainly. I'm so glad.

 SILHOUETTE BOOKS

ISBN 0-373-19362-9

WES STRYKER'S WRANGLED WIFE

Copyright © 1999 by Sandra E. Steffen

Printed in U.S.A.

Books by Sandra Steffen

Silhouette Romance

Child of Her Dreams #1005
*Bachelor Daddy #1028
*Bachelor at the Wedding #1045
*Expectant Bachelor #1056
Lullaby and Goodnight #1074
A Father for Always #1138
For Better, For Baby #1163
†*Luke's Would-Be Bride* #1230
†*Wyatt's Most Wanted Wife* #1241
†*Clayton's Made-Over Mrs.* #1253
†*Nick's Long-Awaited
    Honeymoon* #1290
The Bounty Hunter's Bride #1306
†*Burke's Christmas Surprise* #1337
†*Wes Stryker's Wrangled Wife* #1362

Silhouette Desire

Gift Wrapped Dad #972

Silhouette Special Edition

Not Before Marriage! #1061

Silhouette Books

36 Hours
Marriage by Contract

*Wedding Wager
†Bachelor Gulch

SANDRA STEFFEN

Her fans tell Sandra how much they enjoy her fictional characters, especially her male fictional characters. That's not so surprising, because although this award-winning, bestselling author believes every character is a challenge, she has the most fun with the men she creates, whether they're doctors or cowboys, toddlers or teenagers. Perhaps that's because she's surrounded by so many men—her husband, their four sons, her dad, brothers, in-laws. She feels blessed to be surrounded by just as many warm, intelligent and funny women.

Growing up the fourth child of ten in a family of ambitious and opinionated people, she developed a keen appreciation for laughter and argument, for stubborn people with hearts of gold and intelligent people who aren't afraid of other intelligent people. Sandra lives in Michigan with her husband, three of their sons and a blue-eyed mutt who thinks her name is No-Molly-No. Sandra's book, *Child of Her Dreams,* won the 1994 National Readers' Choice Award. Several of her titles have appeared on national bestseller lists.

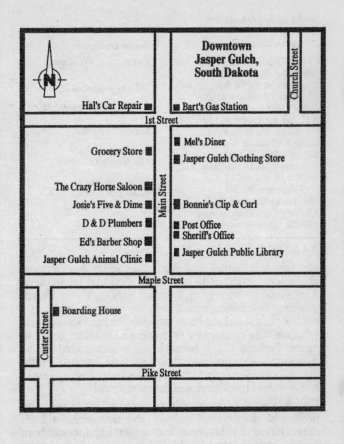

Downtown Jasper Gulch, South Dakota

Church Street

Hal's Car Repair ■ ■ Bart's Gas Station

1st Street

Grocery Store ■

■ Mel's Diner

■ Jasper Gulch Clothing Store

Main Street

The Crazy Horse Saloon ■

Josie's Five & Dime ■ ■ Bonnie's Clip & Curl

D & D Plumbers ■ ■ Post Office

■ Sheriff's Office

Ed's Barber Shop ■

Jasper Gulch Animal Clinic ■ ■ Jasper Gulch Public Library

Maple Street

Custer Street

■ Boarding House

Pike Street

Chapter One

Wes Stryker spread the crinkled sheet of paper out on the small table in front of him. The words, written in fountain-pen ink in an old woman's shaky scrawl, swirled before his eyes. He blinked to bring them into focus, although he knew them by heart. Annabell wanted him to take the kids. Kate and Dusty's kids. The thought of Kate and Dusty, and the accident that had taken their lives, sent a stabbing pain all the way through him.

The blinking lights on the Christmas tree in the corner reflected off his glass of beer. Very festive. Ho. Ho. Ho. Wes folded the letter and very carefully slid it into his pocket. Now and then one or two of the local ranchers who were huddled in the bar made an attempt at small talk, and every five minutes Forest Wilkie deposited more coins in the jukebox. Wes wondered how many times he'd heard Elvis Presley's rendition of ''Blue Christmas'' tonight. Five? Six? It didn't matter, because he was pretty sure that if he heard it one more time, he was going to have to hit somebody.

"Slow night," Butch Brunner mumbled from a table nearby.

Wes acknowledged the statement, but he didn't look up from the beer in front of him. It was a slow night, all right. Christmas Eve. The longest, slowest, dreariest night of the year.

"Snow's really coming down out there."

Wes cast a cursory glance out the window. "Yeah."

"You doin' anything tomorrow?"

"Nope. You?"

"Nope."

Silence. Ah, blessed silence. Unfortunately, it only lasted until Forest deposited more coins.

"For cryin' out loud," one of the other area ranchers grumbled. "Can't you play anything else?"

Ignoring the criticism, Forest settled himself back at his table. Wes continued staring into his beer, wondering what a down-on-his-luck ex-rodeo champion with a bum knee could offer his dead best friends' kids. Children, especially orphaned children, needed a woman's touch, didn't they? He could think of at least one down-on-his-luck ex-rodeo champion who could have used the same thing.

All in all, he figured he'd done a halfway decent job reminding himself that life wasn't so bad. So what if the woman he'd set his sights on had just married somebody else? He liked Louetta Graham. He'd even go so far as to say he liked her a lot, but he hadn't been in love with her. Good ol' Louetta had known it and had proceeded to let him down in a manner that had left his pride intact. And so what if his rodeo days were over? He'd given bronco riding everything he had. The last couple of years, *that* had become harder and harder to do. Wes knew timing was everything—it was one of the reasons he'd taken so many trophies over the years. And it had been time to get out. Start over. Come home.

That was what he'd done.

It wasn't as if he didn't have anything to come home to. He had the ranch, such as it was. Aside from stiff joints and a limp that probably wouldn't be getting a whole lot better, he had his health. He supposed he might as well be thankful that he had the town of Jasper Gulch to come back to, not to mention the Crazy Horse Saloon where he could nurse a beer along with a handful of other men who had no better place to be on Christmas Eve. Now, if Forest would stop playing that danged song, they all might make it through the long, gloomy night.

With that in mind, Wes picked up his beer and downed a good portion of it. Wiping his mouth on the back of his hand, he realized that what he needed was some excitement. A barroom brawl or a warm, willing woman. An intense game of poker or a warm, willing woman. Unfortunately, women were hard to come by in Jasper Gulch, South Dakota. Since the men weren't in the mood to play poker, and the fact that Forest had played "Blue Christmas" seven— good grief, make that eight—times in a row wasn't really a good enough reason to start a barroom brawl, Wes placed his glass on the table and continued to stare into what was left of his beer.

Suddenly the sleigh bells, hanging from the back of the door, jangled up a storm. It wasn't surprising that every man in the room glanced up at the commotion, and it stood to reason that each and every one of those men would perk up considerably. After all, the person who'd entered was a woman, and a damned attractive one, at that. Wes, however, was the only man in the room who didn't duck back behind the safety of his beer. He happened to think their reactions were mighty interesting, not to mention worthy of a little healthy speculation on his part. Evidently the area bachelors knew something he didn't.

Mighty interesting, indeed.

Wes waited to rise to his feet until after the woman had read the card the bar's owners had left on the counter, a card wishing everyone a merry Christmas and a drink or two if they wanted to help themselves. Hooking his fingers loosely over the top of his glass, he moseyed a little closer, reaching the row of bar stools about the same time the woman carried a long-necked brown bottle to the counter and started to wiggle out of her coat.

Holy-moly. Now there was a sight for sore eyes, not to mention a sure cure for boredom. And this was a lot better than a game of poker or a barroom brawl.

He'd seen women in leather coats and suede coats with fringe. He'd seen them in plastic rain slickers and wool and fleece and down-filled jackets. Once he'd even kissed a woman who was wearing mink from head to toe, but he'd never seen a coat quite like the one sliding from this woman's shoulders. He couldn't tell what it was made of. This close, he only knew it was fuzzy looking and had what appeared to be red and purple reindeer, some upside down, some right side up, prancing across it.

She hooked a foot on the bottom rung of the bar stool closest to her and hoisted herself onto the seat. Like a man in a trance, Wes watched as she made herself comfortable. He had a hazy impression of long legs encased in dark brown jeans, ankle-high boots, slight hips and round breasts, recently chilled. In his younger days, Wes would have been tempted to chew on his fist. At thirty-five, he realized there was more to a woman than a good body. It just so happened that once a man got past this particular woman's truly amazing body, he could spend an equal amount of time on her face, which was exactly what he was doing when he found himself looking into electric blue eyes that were looking right back at him.

Coming to his senses enough to realize that it wasn't polite to stare, and because he still considered himself a gentleman, no matter where his gaze had gotten stuck and his thoughts had wandered, he removed his cowboy hat with his left hand and said, "Evening, ma'am."

The only indication she gave that she'd heard him was a slight lift of one perfectly arched black eyebrow. Since it was all the encouragement he needed, what with the way the blood was zinging through his body, he sidled a little closer. "Mind if I sit down?"

She took her time looking him up and down. Seemingly altogether unfazed by his rapt attention, she raised the beer bottle halfway to her lips. "On one condition," she said, holding the bottle in midair.

Wes hitched his weight to one foot and settled his hand, hat and all, to one hip. He waited as long as he could and finally said, "You care to name your condition, or do you want me to guess?"

She eyed the tilt of his head and the half-empty glass held loosely in his right hand, only to catch him red-handed, or red-eyed, or whatever a woman called it when she caught a man peering below her shoulders. Shoot. He wouldn't blame her if she gave him the boot. "Sorry, ma'am. I don't mean to stare. It's just that I don't believe I've ever laid eyes on a woman as exotic looking as you."

She appeared totally unaffected by the compliment. Worse, she looked bored, but she did finally say, "Take a picture. It'll last longer. For the record, in order for me to be exotic looking, my eyes would have to be green, not blue."

Wes disagreed, but was too intrigued to argue. "About that condition you mentioned."

With a shudder, she motioned toward the jukebox. "If you'd ask that man in the brown cowboy hat to play something other than 'Blue Christmas,' you'd be doing me a huge favor. I mean, isn't Christmas depressing enough?"

Wes felt a hundred-watt grin coming on. A woman after

his own heart. Placing his beer and cowboy hat in the empty space next to her, he turned on his heel and dug deep into his pockets for change.

Jayne Kincaid lowered her beer to the counter, untouched. She didn't mind the curiosity coursing through her, but she had a far-too-difficult time dragging her eyes away from the seat of the cowboy's pants. Rats. Her peace of mind was in serious trouble. The man would have been on the tall side even without the scuffed heels of his worn cowboy boots. He was wearing a plain green shirt, the cuffs rolled up, the collar open. Like most of the other men she'd met out here, he wore very little in the way of adornment. No gold chains, certainly no earrings. This cowboy didn't even sport the usual eighteen-pound belt buckle. His belt was plain brown leather, and held up a pair of low-slung blue jeans. At least they'd probably been blue once. Now they were faded, the knees and fly nearly white. For heaven's sake. What was she doing looking at his fly?

Until she'd arrived in this godforsaken town, where her brother had chosen to set up his new medical practice, she hadn't given much thought to cowboy brawn. But she couldn't help wondering where this particular cowboy had gotten the little hitch in his stride. Not that she was interested. Oh, no. She didn't care if his hair did have at least four shades of brown, every one lighter than the last, or that his voice held just enough Western drawl to be interesting. She'd sworn off men for good this time, and from the looks of things, in the nick of time.

She forced her eyes away about the same time coins jangled into the jukebox. Within seconds the twangiest country-western song she'd ever heard wafted through the air.

"Better?" he asked, joining her at the bar.

"Whoever that musician is, I'm a huge fan."

He slid onto the stool with the ease of a man who was

accustomed to spending time in bars. "This guy's been dead for twenty years, but I'm a fan of the yodel, myself. You really are a woman after my own heart."

Through the mirror behind the bar, she assessed the other patrons sitting at various tables throughout the room. It didn't take long to size them up as lonely hearts, not troublemakers. The man sitting next to her wasn't quite so easy to categorize. She lifted the bottle to her mouth and took a small swallow. Licking the taste of foam and barley from her lips, she said, "I'm not after your heart, cowboy. I'm not after anything, not from you, not from anyone."

Wes took a moment to digest the information, then slowly extended his right hand. "You can call me cowboy if you want to, but my name's Wes Stryker."

"I know."

"You know?"

She took another drink, shrugged. "Cletus McCully pointed you out to me at Burke and Louetta's wedding earlier. You owe the man a dollar for all the praises he sang. Unfortunately he wasted his breath. Oh, my name's Jayne Kincaid."

"I know."

She watched him closely, then slowly shook her head. "Cletus McCully?"

Wes rested his forearms along the bar's smooth surface, swirling the beer in his glass while thoughts swirled in his head. Leaning closer, he whispered, "It seems he sang a few of your praises to me, too. He mentioned that you like men with blue eyes. Forgive me for pointing out the obvious, but mine are blue."

Jayne would have liked to be able to dismiss the whole topic with a quick, unaffected glance at his face. But his wasn't the kind of face that allowed easy dismissals or quick glances. His four-shades-of-brown hair was brushed straight back. There were two long lines in his forehead, from concentrating or scowling, she couldn't tell. His eyebrows were thick and had been bleached nearly blond. And he was right. His eyes were blue, and it just so happened that they were the kind of eyes a woman could lose herself in if she wasn't careful. From now on Jayne planned to be very careful.

"Look," she said. "You seem like a nice enough guy, but you're wasting your time. I *was* partial to blue eyes once. My ex-husband has blue eyes."

Jayne watched for a sign that he'd accepted the fact that she just plain wasn't interested. He appeared to be studying the warm beer in his glass. After a long stretch of silence, he cupped his chin in his hand and turned to look at her. Touching his glass to her bottle of beer, he said, "To blue eyes, yours and mine, and to Christmas Eve."

"Christmas Eve," she said with a shudder. "The longest night of the year."

Wes saw a spark of some indefinable emotion in Jayne's eyes. It hinted of battle scars and kindred spirits, and it made him even more curious. "You don't have much in the way of family, either?" he asked. Why else would she be spending Christmas Eve in a hole-in-the-wall bar with a garish Christmas tree in one corner and a mechanical bull strung with white lights in another?

To his surprise she said, "Oh, I have tons of family. Besides my brother, Burke, and my brand-new sister-in-law, Louetta, and little Alex, I have one half brother, two half sisters, oodles of stepbrothers and stepsisters, two parents, several sets of stepparents, one—" she cocked her head at him "—blue-eyed ex-husband and a partridge in a pear tree."

She lifted her beer to her lips again, shrugging as if her brand of humor wasn't unusual. In actuality, there was nothing ordinary about her. Her hair looked thick, the tendrils surrounding her face blunt-edged, the rest unruly. The style shouldn't have looked so damned pretty, when *pretty* was the last word he would use to describe her. *Exotic, gorgeous, sexy.* Now those were words that were synonymous with Jayne Kincaid. He noticed that her hands were soft and smooth looking, and he wondered what she did for a living. She knew her way around a bar, but she was no barfly. And no matter how much family she claimed to have, she didn't have any better place to be on Christmas Eve than he did.

"Do you want to get out of here?" he said. "Maybe go for a drive?"

Or back to my place? went unsaid between them.

Jayne came out of her double take shaking her head. She was thirty-two years old, and she'd been away from the game for a long time. She was rusty, and she planned to stay that way. "Look," she said, "I don't mean to sound cold or impersonal, but I'm not looking for a relationship. I'm not even looking for a fling. I'm finished with men."

"You're going to let one loser taint your view of all men?" he asked.

"First of all, my husband wasn't a loser. And secondly, my view of men isn't tainted." Jayne nearly bristled. She hadn't meant to sound as if she wasn't completely over Sherman. Maybe she wasn't, but she didn't want anybody's pity.

"Then you don't really dislike us?" he asked with a half smile.

Good grief. She couldn't believe she was having this conversation. All she'd wanted to do was get out of the house for a little while. Oh, Burke and Louetta had both assured her that she was welcome to spend the evening with them, but this was their wedding night, and there were just some things that sisters, particularly newly divorced sisters, were better off not witnessing or hearing or imagining.

"Look," she finally said, "I dislike a few, but no, I don't

dislike all men. I'm just not going to get attached to any
more of you, that's all.''

"You're not?"

"No, I'm not." Raising one hand, she began listing on
her fingers all the benefits to remaining single. "No more
wondering if a man is really attending a business meeting
at 1:00 a.m. No more picking up heavy suits from the dry
cleaners. No more rushing home from work to spend time
with a man who's made other plans for the evening. No
more trying to appease an unappeasable man, or understand
an irrational one, or try to plan a meal around a picky man's
tastes. I can eat chicken seven days a week if I want to. I
can sleep in the middle of the bed, and there are no whisk-
ers in my sinks. I don't need a man to define me, and I can
open my own jars, thank you very much. And perhaps best
of all, the toilet seats are always down.''

Jayne almost felt smug. Festive, that's what she felt.
Buoyant. She'd never put it into words before, and it
sounded good. It *felt* good. She truly didn't dislike men. At
least not most of them. She loved her brother, her half
brother and stepbrothers and nephew, and her father, and
stepfathers, although she had issues with a few of them.
Men had interesting voices and broad shoulders and com-
ical habits. But she *didn't* need a man to define her. She
didn't need a man for anything.

"Jayne?"

She turned her head at the sound of her name. While
she'd been lost in thought, Wes had inched closer. She
could see the tiny lines feathering his eyes, the crease lining
one lean cheek, the light brown whisker stubble on his
cheeks and jaw. His eyes held her spellbound, his gaze
dipping to her mouth and back again as he said, "What
about sex?"

The song on the jukebox ended, causing the entire room
to become so quiet a person could have heard a pin drop.

All Jayne could hear was the pounding in her ears, and the catch in her voice as she asked, "What about it?"

He leaned in, slow and easy. "Are you planning to do without that for the rest of your life, too?"

The deep timbre of his voice reminded her of a guitar string stretched tight and slowly strummed. She had no doubt the man could sweet-talk with the best of them. She should know. She'd been sweet-talked by pros. She'd also been lied to and cheated on and tossed aside, and not only by her ex-husband.

In the background, coins jangled into the jukebox. Within seconds the first strains of "Blue Christmas" started all over again.

She could feel Wes Stryker's eyes on her. She knew she could have said something blunt and sassy to put him in his place, but for some reason she didn't. It was his eyes. The rest of him exuded smugness, but those blue eyes of his were tinged with sadness. The man had troubles, and she didn't see any reason to add to them. She picked up the bottle in front of her and took a hardy swallow.

"Well?" he prodded.

"Sex," she said, reaching for her coat and sliding off the stool, "is highly overrated."

She held up her hand, anticipating his protest. "Trust me on this, Wes. Or simply agree that we disagree. Oh, and merry Christmas." Without another word she walked to the door, gave it a yank and strode out into the cold.

The room remained quiet until the last bell hanging on the hook on the back of the door had stopped jingling. And then it seemed that every spectator had something to say.

"Oooo-eee," Butch Brunner exclaimed. "That woman's definitely an eyeful."

"She is that," Forest agreed. "But she'll give you an earful without even trying."

"Why," one of the other men said, "she practically

singed the hair in the ears of every man in the diner the first time she set foot in the place.''

"I don't think she's the kind of woman the Carson brothers had in mind when they decided to advertise for women to come to Jasper Gulch a few years back.''

"No sirree, Bob.''

Wes listened, but he didn't add to the conversation flowing through the saloon. An eyeful? An earful? He'd bet his last trophy she'd be a handful in bed.

The woman had certainly packed a wallop in the short amount of time she'd spent in the Crazy Horse. He'd known people who talked for hours but said less than Jayne Kincaid had said with two words, a wry twist of her lips and a slight thrust of her chin. She'd been married, divorced and hurt. And she *thought* she wasn't looking for a man. Wes happened to believe that everyone was looking for a partner, the other half of a whole, someone to share this messy journey humans called life. And sex wasn't overrated, no matter what she'd said. It was one of life's most pleasurable, not to mention its most powerful, driving forces. It was like a tidal wave or a hurricane or the rotation of the earth around the sun. A man could ignore it, but he couldn't pretend it didn't exist.

And neither could Jayne Kincaid.

Jayne Kincaid. He let her name roll around in his mind, along with the image of her sky blue eyes and that cockamamy way she wore her short, dark hair. Butch was right. She had a helluva body. Yet she did nothing to draw attention to it or detract from it. She wasn't a flirty little rodeo bunny or a city-wise coquette or an ice queen, for that matter. This was a warm-blooded woman who knew the ropes and wouldn't hesitate to hang a man on them. Dang. Women like that were few and far between.

Merry Christmas, she'd said. Wes still wasn't sure about the merry part, but it had turned out to be an interesting

Christmas Eve, that was for sure. He rose to his feet slowly. Taking his time buttoning his sheepskin jacket, he wondered how long he should wait before he paid her a little visit.

"Ya leaving, Wes?" Forest called gloomily from the back of the room.

"Yeah. I think I'll call it a night." Wes said goodbye to the men who were still huddled inside the Crazy Horse Saloon. Whether any of them noticed or not, he was feeling a sight more amicable leaving the bar than he'd been going in. Even the sting of the wind and the blinding snow didn't dampen his mood. He simply punched on the lights, turned up the heat and switched on the windshield wipers in his shiny silver truck. He was halfway home when he noticed that he was whistling to a Christmas song about a rusty Chevrolet. It had been a long time since he'd felt like whistling about anything.

His first glimpse of the dilapidated fence posts lining his driveway drew the whistle from his lips. The rundown old house had little appeal in the light of day. At night, it was downright depressing. He should have remembered to turn a light on before he left. Not that he was accustomed to being greeted by lighted windows. It was just that this was the first Christmas Eve he'd spent on the ranch since he'd buried his father a few years back. And it was the first Christmas Eve to come and go since Dusty and Kate had died.

Wes pulled his fancy pickup truck into the barn and got out. The bucking bronco emblem on the doors had been Dusty's idea. It seemed that Carlin "Dusty" Malone had always had some grand scheme up his sleeve, most of which had gotten the two of them into trouble.

Wes closed the heavy barn door, latched it and headed for the house. He was chilled by the time he shut the back door behind him, but although his knee ached a little, he didn't experience that knife-in-the-gut feeling thoughts of Dusty usually evoked. Tonight the memory of Dusty's crooked smile made Wes smile a little himself.

He hung his hat and coat on a hook by the door, ran a hand through his hair and wandered to the bedroom where he'd spent most of his youth planning his escape from Jasper Gulch. His leaving hadn't bothered his father. By that time, Sam Stryker's only love was for the bottle he curled up with every night, and maybe the fleeting memory of the woman he'd buried when Wes had been five.

Wes barely remembered his mother, but he'd always thought she would have liked Dusty Malone. He and Dusty had started on the rodeo circuit the same year. Dusty had ridden bulls, while bucking broncos had been Wes's specialty. Nothing had come between them, not winning, or losing, not barroom brawls, not even falling for the same girl. When that girl had married Dusty, Wes had been the best man. Although Dusty had insisted that *he* would always be the best man, Wes had always known that Dusty would have done the same for him if the tables had been turned and Kate had married him, instead. Friends like that didn't come along every day. Kate used to say that all the time. She also used to say she'd married one of the only two men on the planet who put the toilet seat down. Obviously, putting the toilet seat down was a big deal with women. It had certainly been an issue with Jayne Kincaid.

Wes's right boot hit the floor about the same time thoughts of Jayne Kincaid jump-started his heart. He took the letter out of his pocket and placed it on the stand next to his bed. He knew he had a decision to make regarding Dusty's two kids, but it wasn't the kids he was thinking about as he turned back the covers. He was thinking about Jayne, and he wished to high heaven he wasn't crawling into bed alone.

* * *

Wes opened his eyes slowly. He wasn't sure what had awakened him. It wasn't quite daybreak, but it was close, the color of the sky on the other side of his wavy windowpanes somewhere between black and gray. He felt a smile pulling at his face, not because it was Christmas—he didn't have a tree or even a stocking, after all—but because he had a woman on his mind. That's what had awakened him. He'd been dreaming, and while the remnants of the dream weren't clear in his mind, they were evident on his body.

He wondered if Jayne was awake yet. And he wondered what she would say if he called on her so early in the day. While he was at it, he wondered how she would react if he told her he was going to petition for guardianship of Kate and Dusty's two kids and raise them the best way he knew how. Would she say he was nuts? Maybe he was. But other than their father's eighty-two-year-old great aunt, Annabell, who lived in a two-bedroom house southeast of Sioux Falls, two hundred and twenty miles away, and Kate's long-lost sister who could be dead for all anybody knew, Wes was all those two kids had.

He made quick use of the facilities, layered on his clothes and hiked out to the kitchen. Shivering, he made a mental note of all the things he had to do to get the place ready for Logan and Olivia's arrival. He could have lived in the barn, but a five-year-old girl and her ten-year-old brother needed heat and windows with glass instead of plywood. They needed good food in their stomachs. Most of all they needed to know he wanted them.

Picking up the old black telephone from the place it had sat for as long as he could remember, he dialed the number Annabell had listed in her letter. Her answering machine clicked on after the fourth ring. Wes smiled, remembering some of the messages she'd left on that thing. Most folks her age didn't even bother with the contraptions, but Annabell Malone wasn't like most folks her age. She welcomed challenges, and wasn't afraid to try new things. For an eighty-two-year-old woman she was very young at heart.

Figuring they were all probably in church, Wes followed the instructions Annabell recited in her feeble-sounding voice and left a message. He took a minute to start the coffee, then donned his sheepskin jacket and his favorite cowboy hat. At the last minute, he went in search of the cellular phone. Tucking it into his pocket just in case Annabell returned his call any time soon, he headed outside to feed and water the horses.

Maybe he'd hook the trailer up to his truck and haul Stomper and the sleigh into town in a little while. He was in the process of imagining Jayne's reaction to such an old-fashioned activity when he lowered his right foot to the first step.

Whoosh.

He was airborne. His arms flailed, his feet flew out from under him. He landed on the icy ground five steps below, in less time than it had taken High Kicker to buck him off that time down in Santa Fe. He was gasping for breath and in too much pain to be dead, so the fall couldn't have killed him. He couldn't tell if he'd damaged the ribs that had started to heal, and his knee was aching pretty badly again, but it was the searing pain in his left shoulder that kept him very still. Damn. He'd dislocated it again.

Clutching his shoulder with both hands, he picked up one boot, gritted his teeth and tried to roll onto his side. His foot slid on the ice, his bad knee crashing onto the hard surface so fast he saw stars. He tried rolling the other way, but he almost passed out from the pain slicing through his shoulder. He tried several other maneuvers. The results were the same.

He should have known his father wouldn't have had the downspout fixed, thereby routing the rainwater to a less hazardous spot. From the look of the place and the back taxes that had to be paid, it was obvious that his father hadn't taken care of much of anything these past several years. It looked as if it was up to him to make the place operational again. First, he had to figure out a way to get up.

Think, Stryker, think.

He considered whistling for Stomper, but Wes had closed the stall door himself yesterday, and although Stomper could finagle an apple or a carrot out of anybody's pocket, he wouldn't be able to unlatch the stall. It was fifteen miles to town, two miles to his nearest neighbor. It was also Christmas morning, and not too many people would be out and about, and if they were, they wouldn't be driving past this old place on Old Stump Road.

Wes was breathing easier and thinking clearly. A lot of good it did him. Between the ice and the pain, he was stuck on his back, staring at a sky as dull as the old steel sink in his kitchen, cold seeping into his coat and jeans as he tried to decide how to keep from freezing to death. His fingers were already starting to tingle. He slid them into his pockets, paused. What the—

He took a careful breath and he almost smiled.

Lo and behold, the cellular phone.

Chapter Two

"Look, Alex! A truck! And a doctor's kit. Can you tell Aunt Jayne thank you?"

"Tanks, Aun'ie Jayne. Aun'ie Jayne!"

"Jayne?"

"Sis, are you all right?"

"What?" Jayne came out of her musings with a start, only to find Louetta, Burke and Alex staring at her from the living room floor where wrapping paper and ribbons were strewn everywhere.

"Alex said thanks," Burke said, watching her closely.

"Oh, you're very welcome, Alex."

Alex went back to his new truck, but Burke and Louetta continued looking at her strangely. Normally, it wouldn't have bothered Jayne. People looked at her strangely all the time, but Burke and Louetta looked concerned, and that made Jayne uneasy.

"You were a thousand miles away," Burke said, handing Alex another package.

Jayne pulled a face.

"Is everything all right?" he asked, obviously reluctant to let the subject drop.

"My mind wandered, that's all."

"Were you daydreaming or reminiscing?" Louetta asked in that quiet, knowing way she had.

Unwilling to admit just how close Louetta had come to the truth, Jayne stifled a yawn and gestured to the two-year-old, who was tearing into another package with obvious glee. The ploy worked: Burke's and Louetta's attention strayed to Alex and then met over the top of his dark, little head. Louetta was wearing a pale pink robe she'd bought especially for her new husband, and although Burke had pulled on a cable-knit sweater and a pair of navy chinos, they were obviously having a difficult time keeping their hands off each other. They'd been married less than a day, which made the open longing in their expressions perfectly understandable.

Jayne was happy for them, but she felt restless. She had last night, too. She'd slept with a pillow over her head to muffle the constant sigh of the wind. She yawned again because she hadn't slept well, and she couldn't blame it entirely on the wind.

This was just great. She hadn't had an honest-to-goodness dream in over three years, and then out of the blue, last night's sleep had been filled with hazy, erotic images of spurs and lassos and hair four shades of brown. One of her closest friends back in Seattle happened to be a therapist, and would have been intrigued, although what Jayne had been doing to that pillow upon awakening might have made the by-the-book therapist's blue blood turn as bronze as the naked chest in her dreams.

Oh, for heaven's sake, she thought as warmth inched through her body. It wasn't as if she'd actually done any of the things she'd dreamed she was doing. Er, that is, she hadn't *really* slid a rope around Wes Stryker's shoulders and drawn him to her, hand-over-hand, and she certainly hadn't...

She jerked her attention back to the present and caught Burke looking at her again. She didn't want him to worry. After all the agony he and Louetta had both suffered these past two and a half years they'd been apart, they deserved every bit of happiness they were experiencing.

Although she and Burke didn't share many physical characteristics, other than their dark hair, their stubborn streaks were evenly matched. She'd planned to spend Christmas morning in her room, but he'd insisted, in no uncertain terms, that nobody was going to open a package until Jayne had joined them at the tree. So she'd pulled a brush through her short hair and quickly pulled on the first skirt and sweater she'd come to in the tiny closet. She'd joined Burke, Louetta and Alex for the Christmas-morning chaos, watching from a distance, in the room, but not too close to the tight little circle the new family was quickly forming.

She tried not to recall all the Christmases she'd spent just outside the warm glow of *real* family. Strangely, another kind of warm glow kept filtering into her mind.

The phone rang in the kitchen, bringing Jayne back to reality with a jolt. She was on her feet, relieved to have something constructive to do, and was halfway to the kitchen before the second ring. Grabbing the receiver, she said, "Dr. Kincaid's residence."

For a moment there was only silence, and then a deep, husky voice reached her ear through the phone line. "It just dawned on me that this is exactly the way you sounded in my dreams last night. Breathless and full of restless energy."

Her ear tingled, and she felt a strange fluttering sensation where her heart used to be before it had twirled down into her stomach. "Who is this?" She knew, but Wes didn't need to know that.

"I'm hurt."

"I'll bet."

"No, really. I'm hurt. I fell."

"Oh, my God. I'll get Burke."

"No. Jayne. Wait. I was a little afraid I'd freeze to death, but the sound of your voice is working wonders in that department."

She smelled a rat. Turning her back on the intimate little scene in the next room, she said, "What's going on, Stryker?"

"I need you to come out to the ranch and help me up."

"Excuse me?"

He chuckled. "You sound very suspicious and very sexy, and for the record, I don't need help for what you're thinking."

"You couldn't possibly know what I'm thinking."

"Wanna bet?"

"It's all in your mind."

"It was all in my dreams last night. *You* were in my dreams last night."

She wished he would stop mentioning dreams. "What do you really want, Wes?"

"That's a question I wouldn't mind discussing at great length, but for now, I slipped on some ice. I didn't know the snow had turned to sleet over night. You could say I discovered it the hard way. Anyway, I'm stuck on my back like a turtle. My shoulder's dislocated, and the ice, my bad knee and the ribs I busted a few months back have rendered me immobile for the time being."

Jayne's mind reeled. "Dammit, Wes, why didn't you say so? Burke! Come quick!"

She could hear Wes protesting as she handed the phone

to her brother. "It's Wes Stryker. It seems he's fallen. We should call an ambulance."

Burke took the phone. After a few pointed questions and a series of *Uh-huh*s and *I see*s, he covered the mouthpiece with one hand and spoke softly to Jayne. "He says he doesn't need an ambulance, and I believe him."

"But..."

Burke shrugged. "I know it sounds strange, but most of the ranchers and cowboys I've treated out here can diagnose their conditions as well as I can. Often the examination is just a technicality. Wes says all he needs is a helping hand getting to his feet. He'd like that someone to be you."

Jayne glanced at Louetta as if to ask if the cowboy was for real and if he could be trusted. At Louetta's small nod, Jayne shook her head. "I don't believe this." Yanking the phone out of her brother's hand, she said, "If I find candlesticks and a table set for two, you're dead meat, Stryker."

When his deep, throaty chuckle reached her ear, she muttered something very unladylike, slammed the phone down and reached for her keys, sputtering under her breath that he was going to get her help, all right. And then he was going to get a piece of her mind.

Jayne hated country roads. Given a choice, she'd take a five-lane freeway during rush-hour traffic over these curving back roads that were chock-full of chatter bumps and potholes. Burke had wanted to drive her to Wes's place, but she'd wanted to come alone. For reasons she preferred not to explore, she'd needed to escape the intimate atmosphere in her brother's house on Custer Street.

She glanced at her car phone, turned the defroster up a notch and blew a lock of hair out of her eyes. Who in their right mind would set up a medical practice on Custer Street, anyway? Custer died, big-time, didn't he? The names of some of the roads she'd taken this morning weren't much better, but it was the layer of ice covering them that made them truly treacherous, which was why the fifteen-mile trek out to the Double S Ranch had already taken thirty-five minutes. Although it seemed more like forever, Jayne spent the time contemplating what she would say if this was all a hoax and what she would do if it wasn't.

Her fingers cramped from squeezing the steering wheel so hard; her eyes burned from squinting into the sun that had started to shine halfway into the trip. Thankful to have been born with a good sense of direction, she followed the course Louetta had recited, passing sheds and piles of rocks that served as landmarks. It was a relief when she finally found Old Stump Road. Within minutes she pulled into a driveway, her tires sliding to a stop. It required a conscious effort to peel her fingers off the steering wheel. Honestly, if Wes wasn't at least half-dead, he was going to be sorry.

At first glance out of the corner of her eye, she thought she saw him by the barn, but it turned out to be an old barrel. With a sweeping gaze she took in a pair of discarded tires, a roll of rusty wire fence and a stack of hay covered with ice. Shading her eyes with one hand, she peered in the other direction.

Oh, my God, Wes. She froze: her gaze, her mind, everything.

The next thing she knew, she was slipping and sliding up the slight hill that led to the side of the house where a lone figure lay perfectly still, his cowboy hat upside down a few feet away.

"Wes! Are you all right?"

Silence.

"Are you dead? If you're dead I'm never going to forgive you." She was leaning over him now, gazing at a face that had been rugged looking last night but now had a deathly pallor. "Wes, say something. Anything."

His eyes opened slowly, his dark blue irises tinged with gray. "Honey, I didn't know you cared."

She sputtered the same four-letter word she'd used at Burke and Louetta's earlier. One corner of Wes's mouth lifted in a half smile. "And to think you eat out of that mouth. Really, I love it when a woman talks dirty to me, but I'd enjoy it more if I were mobile, if you don't mind."

If he hadn't tried to roll over, the action having elicited a pain-filled groan that made her wince and him swear, she would have told him what he could do with his mobility. "Dammit, Wes. I knew I should have called an ambulance."

His face relaxed, his eyes closing. "I hate ambulances. Besides, I don't need an ambulance. I need you."

Her silence must have drawn his attention, because he looked up at her and said, "What, no scathing comeback?"

Hesitating, she measured him for a moment. "I was just wondering how hard you hit your head."

"Don't worry. My ribs and shoulder took the brunt of the fall."

"And you're sure nothing's broken?"

"As sure as I can be at this point. What are you doing?"

A moment later she'd shrugged out of her fire-engine red coat and very carefully slid it underneath his head. Wes couldn't come up with a reasonable explanation for the warmth that suddenly wrapped around him. He only knew he wanted to pull Jayne down on top of him and explore this living, breathing thing that had started to come to life the moment she'd set foot inside the Crazy Horse last night.

"Jayne, you'll freeze."

She stood up and promptly began to slide down the gradual decline. Slowly making her way back to Wes, she said, "Only if you don't shut up and help me figure out a way to get you to your feet."

"There's a can of ground coffee sitting on the counter."

"You want me to make coffee? *Now?*"

He almost grinned. "The coffee's already made. I was thinking that maybe we could use the coffee in the can for traction."

"Traction," she said, a dawning look of realization crossing her features a split second before she rose carefully to her feet. "Of course we need traction. Something for me to stand on to get a foothold, and something for you to use to keep from slipping. Don't move. I'll be right back."

Since Wes couldn't move, he did as she said. He watched her until she half slid, half skated beyond his peripheral vision, listening intently to the sound of her footsteps and the string of expletives she muttered when she almost fell. The screen door creaked open, followed by a stretch of silence Wes couldn't measure. And then she was back, a can of salt in one hand, his brand-new tin of coffee in the other. She sprinkled them both on the ground all around him, taking extra care to grind the concoction into the ice. Seemingly satisfied that neither she nor Wes would slip as long as they were careful, she glided down to her knees.

"Do you think you can move now?" she asked.

Wes gritted his teeth, bent both knees and rolled to his side. Her hands circled his upper arm, flitting to his back and down around his waist as if she didn't know where to put them. He wouldn't have minded the opportunity to enjoy this. Unfortunately it required all his concentration to keep from passing out as he pushed himself to his knees. Stars flashed before his eyes. Pain shot through his shoulder, biting, searing, cutting. His ears were ringing by the time he found his feet, and sweat had broken out on his upper lip.

He took a few moments to catch his breath. When the world came back into focus, he held his left arm close to his body and staggered two steps.

"Wes, where are you going?"

He started to slip, jerked, then regained his balance. "Help me get closer to the house."

She did as he said.

"Okay, now stand back."

"What are you going to—"

He closed his eyes and slammed his shoulder against the siding. There was a roaring din in his ears and unbearable pain. He heard Jayne swear, but as if from a great distance. Moment by moment, inch by inch, the pain drained out of him, the blood slowly returning to his head. He opened his eyes, tried his shoulder and slanted her a cocky grin. "There. I'm as good as new."

She seethed.

"Next time you decide to body slam a house, would you give me a little warning?"

"I'm hoping there isn't going to be a next time." Being careful not to put all his weight on his bad knee, he tested it. Satisfied that it wouldn't give out on him, he took a shuddering breath and checked his ribs. Although a couple of them ached, he didn't think they were broken.

"Well?"

The edge in Jayne's voice brought his head around and his eyes open. She was looking at him, her chin raised slightly, her lush lips pursed haughtily, despite the way she was shivering.

Aw, she was shivering. Of course she was shivering, he thought, coming to his senses. She wasn't wearing a coat. She *was* wearing a high-necked sweater and a skirt in bold colors that nobody in their right mind would put together. And yet on her it looked good. Maybe it was the fit, not the style—he bent over, stiffly scooping his hat off the ground, then proceeded to take a step toward her—or maybe she would look good no matter what she was wearing. Or wasn't wearing.

Jayne didn't know what to make of the expression on

Wes's face, but the careful, deliberate way he was walking toward her had masculine intent written all over it. She would have backed up, except her feet seemed to be frozen to the ground. Only her eyes had the ability to move, and they were trained on the man who was advancing with quiet purpose.

"What do you think you're—"

Without warning, he bent at the waist, snagged her coat from the ground and very carefully placed it on her shoulders. There was warmth in the hand resting lightly on the back of her neck. Another kind of warmth darkened the color of his eyes as he said, "What did you think I was going to do?"

She relaxed her shoulders, but not her guard. Not one to invite trouble, she refrained from telling him that if she were a betting woman, she would have laid ten-to-one odds that he was going to kiss her.

He stared at her through narrowed eyes and slowly eased closer. Make that a-hundred-to-one odds. His face hovered inches from hers, not close enough to kiss her, after all, but close enough to make her slightly uncomfortable and very aware. Of him as a man and of herself as a woman, and of what the two of them could do together. It made her wonder if his chest was really as tanned as it had been in her dreams and if his stomach really had those washboard ripples...

Jayne blinked against the image and told herself to get a grip. What she had to do was get out of there before she did something she would regret. "It's time I was going. I can't say this has been fun, but it has been interesting."

He looked at her long and hard, but he made no reply.

"You are okay, aren't you?"

He turned without a word, heading for the barn.

Jayne had to force her mouth closed and felt herself bristling all over again. Did the man have no manners?

"Driving on those silly old icy roads was no trouble,

really," she called to his back. "There's no need to thank me. It was nothing, honest."

He didn't so much as shrug, although she was sure he looked right at her after he'd unlatched a weathered barn door and had slowly pushed it open far enough to slip through.

The wind was cold at her back, and her feet were freezing inside her thin boots, yet she didn't make a beeline for her car. Something didn't add up. She'd been around men all her life. She'd been yelled at by a few and tiptoed around by several, but men rarely ignored her. Wes Stryker had been a perfect gentleman the previous night, with his "evenin', ma'am" and his slow, easy smile. So what was this silent treatment all about?

She supposed it was curiosity that had her skating toward the barn and slipping inside. "Stryker?" she called, wrinkling her nose at the smell of horses and hay and something she hoped she hadn't already stepped in. "If I ruin this pair of boots, I'm going to hold you personally responsible. Where are you, anyway?"

"I'm right here."

She jumped at his sudden appearance in a doorway a few feet away. When he disappeared again, she followed, striding past a row of dark stalls and into an area that was divided into two sections by a wooden fence. "Why is it," she said as her eyes slowly adjusted to the light spilling through three high windows, "that you only answer half my questions?"

Wes waited to breathe a sigh of relief until after he'd returned the scoop to the barrel of oats. She hadn't left. Hallelujah, she hadn't left.

He'd almost kissed her out in the yard. A tiny thread of self-preservation had stopped him at the last minute, because something had warned him that if he kissed her, she would hightail it out of there. And he didn't want her to leave. He wanted her to stay, and that wanting scared him more than he cared to admit.

Being careful of his left shoulder, he carried the bucket of oats to a far corner and emptied it into the feeder. Three horses immediately started eating. Smoothing his hand over the middle horse's gray muzzle, he said, "I've always been a firm believer in letting actions speak for themselves."

Jayne strolled a little closer, thinking about Wes's answer. She didn't know what to make of him. What, exactly, were his actions saying right now? He was looking at a horse, stroking its muzzle with his right hand. His hand was broad and tanned, his fingers blunt tipped and slightly crooked, as if they'd been broken a time or two. It was a masculine hand, but not a terribly attractive one, and yet there was something very attractive about the way it moved up and down the horse's head.

"Is he your favorite horse?" she asked in a quiet voice.

"He was my best friend's favorite horse."

The current in his voice drew her gaze. "Does he have a name?"

"My friend's name was Dusty. This is Gray."

"How long ago did Dusty die?"

Wes's hand went perfectly still. "How did you know he died?"

She studied him thoughtfully for a moment. He'd done it again, hadn't answered her question. "I guess bleeding hearts recognize each other."

She strolled a little closer, drawing a line in the dust on the top board of the stall with a finger. "I spent the first few months after Sherman moved out wondering if I was going crazy. I couldn't eat, I couldn't sleep, I couldn't concentrate. A friend of mine convinced me to enroll in an art class. Another friend suggested yoga." Jayne shook her head. "I have no artistic talent, and all that breathing and chanting didn't relax me. It drove me crazy. I know death and divorce aren't the same things, but they're both losses. I won't say something trite, trying to minimize your pain, but time has helped me.''

She glanced up from the dust on her finger and found him looking at her. She hadn't realized she'd moved so close to him, and she certainly hadn't intended to tell him about something as personal as her divorce. It was still a touchy subject, but if her experience eased his sorrow in some tiny way, she wasn't sorry she'd bared a small corner of her soul.

''Jayne?''

She stared at him, patiently waiting for him to pour a little of his own heart out to her.

''You were married to a man named Sherman?''

Jayne blinked. She'd unearthed her soul, and his only comment pertained to her ex-husband's name?

Did he have no feelings? Okay, he hadn't laughed, but there had been incredulity in his voice. What? Hadn't he ever known anyone named Sherman? There had been plenty of emotion in his voice when he'd mentioned his best friend. In some perverse way, she was glad he hadn't turned all maudlin on her. Still, it made her curious. Just what was Wes Stryker made of? He was a man—a very private one. She doubted he enjoyed having someone traipse through his thought processes. In that respect he wasn't so different from the men she'd known in Seattle.

The men back home wore expensive suits for work and designer sportswear for play. Wes was wearing a sheepskin jacket, the collar turned up, jeans that had seen better days and a faded shirt that looked as soft as butter. His skin had acquired a permanent tan, and there was whisker stubble on his cheeks and jaw. She'd never been a fan of facial hair and yet his did nothing to detract from the hollows, planes and angles of his rugged face. For all his face's interesting contours, she was most interested in the depth and intensity of his eyes.

Crossing her arms, she said, "You're something else, Stryker, do you know that?"

A smile found its way to his mouth much the way a cloud drifted over the face of the sun. "You're not so bad yourself."

Jayne could count on one hand the times in her life she'd been speechless, and yet in the tight space so near him, she couldn't think of a single thing to do or say. He had no such problem, reaching for her hand as if it was the most natural thing in the world. She'd thought he was going to kiss her earlier. Now she was sure. She knew she should try to fight it, but as he lowered his face, she lifted hers, his features blurring before her eyes, his breath a soft rasp on her cheek, her heartbeat a slow stutter in her chest.

Something streaked past her ankles, fluttering the hem of her skirt. She jerked, shrieked and jumped. Her clamber to the top of the gate might not have been graceful, but it was certainly fast.

A cat hissed. A dog whined. Jayne screamed again.

"It's all right," Wes said. "It was just a cat. Marilyn won't hurt you."

Jayne turned her head slowly. Holding on to the top board with one hand, she peered over her shoulder where a scruffy-looking, half-grown kitten stood in a corner, back arched, fur on end. A dog that must have weighed at least seven times more seemed to be trying to decide how to get closer to the kitten. The kitten swiped and spat, sending the dog reeling backward.

"Come on, Marilyn. Be nice."

Jayne loosened her grip on the gate with utmost care. "You have a problem with my ex-husband's name, and yet you named a kitten Marilyn?"

"I never said I had a problem with your ex-husband's name. What don't you like about 'Marilyn'?"

She used the time it took to get her breathing and heart rate under control to look around. The horses were still eating, Marilyn's back was still arched, and two other kittens were watching from the hayloft. "You have to admit it's an unusual name for a cat. What do you call them?"

He looked over his shoulder, but he didn't turn around.

"The calico one is Carolyn, the butterscotch-colored one is Sherilyn."

Carolyn, Marilyn and Sherilyn? "They're all females?"

"I haven't had the heart to check."

Another time Jayne might have laughed. As it was, she could only shake her head. Being careful not to get her feet tangled up in the folds of her brightly colored skirt, she climbed down from the gate and put a little distance between her and Wes.

One of the horses nickered, and the one named Gray tossed his head and snorted. Marilyn, the kitten, joined her sisters, if they were indeed all females, the dog watching silently.

"It's quite a menagerie of pets you have here, Stryker," she said, pulling up the zipper tab on her coat.

Wes pulled the brim of his cowboy hat lower on his forehead, watching as Jayne prepared to leave. She was putting on a pair of bright green gloves, her lower lip tucked between her teeth. If it hadn't been for two of those pets she'd mentioned, he would have known how her lips felt and tasted.

He wished...

He didn't know what he wished anymore. He only knew that this woman had driven out here when he'd needed her, and he didn't want her to go. Not yet, not until they'd talked a little more and maybe he'd kissed her very thoroughly. Maybe not even then.

"Well," she was saying, backing up. "I guess I'll leave you to your assorted pets."

By the time his gaze made it back to her face, he found her looking at him, waiting for him to say something. During the seventeen years he'd spent on the rodeo circuit he'd made small talk with just about everybody he'd seen, from rodeo clowns to judges to buckle bunnies. And here he was, standing before a woman he wanted to impress, as tongue-tied as a teenager with a new pair of boots and his father's car, trying to work up his courage to talk to the prettiest girl in school.

"You're right about the animals," he finally managed to say as he shortened the distance between them. "They're all misfits in one way or another. By rights, kittens born so late in the year shouldn't have survived. The dog came limping into the barn a week ago, hungry and half-frozen, no collar, no tags. I asked around, but nobody seems to know who he belongs to."

Jayne looked at him and then at the dog. "What's his name?"

Wes shrugged. "I thought I'd wait and see if he decides to stay before I name him."

He wondered if she would say something negative about the animal. He wouldn't have blamed her if she had. The dog was a mongrel, not quite brown, not quite black, ugly by most people's standards. He had a dull coat, a cropped tail and a slight limp, not at all unlike Wes's.

Wes wondered which of those features Jayne would comment on. She leaned down and held out the back of her hand, letting the dog sniff. "He has soulful eyes."

Wes swore the beating rhythm of his heart changed tempo. Nothing about the conversation should have aroused lust, yet his desire for her was strong. The entire time it was wrapping around him, soft-touched thoughts were shaping his smile. "So do you, Jayne. So do you."

He could tell by the way she shook her head very slowly, very precisely and rose stiffly to her feet that he probably shouldn't have said it. But hell, it was true. He strolled closer, intent upon convincing her to stay. She shook her head again. "Look," she said, "just so you don't get the wrong idea. I didn't come out here to start something. I meant what I said last night. I'm finished with men. All men."

"You can't deny the attraction that's between us."

Her eyes narrowed. "Wanna bet?"

He took another step in her direction. He liked the way her chin came up and her shoulders went back. He especially liked the way his blood was heating as it made its way to the very center of him. Ignoring the hand she held up to ward off his advance, he said, "I want you. And I think you want me."

Her blue eyes narrowed, flashing with insolence. "You *must* have hit your head earlier."

"I don't think so."

Looking him up and down in a manner that would have made a lesser man crumble, she said, "If you tell me you have an itch and a hankering, I'll be forced to clobber you."

He eased closer. "That's one way to put it."

"It was the way my ex-husband put it when I confronted him with my suspicions that he was seeing another woman. He said the affair meant nothing, he'd had an itch, that's all, and a hankering. I told him to scratch the itch and shove the hankering. The same goes for you."

She turned on her heel and headed for the door.

Since Wes didn't want her to leave, period, and he especially didn't want her to leave angry, he followed her outside. "Jayne?" he called when she was halfway to her car.

Jayne came to an abrupt stop. Although it went against

her better judgment, she turned around. She found herself looking across the expanse of yard where the barn stood in stark contrast to the snow and the sky. If there had ever been any paint on the old building, it was long gone, the boards weathered to a dull, dark gray. Wes's cowboy hat was gray, too, but a lighter shade, and although she couldn't see his eyes from here, she could feel the intensity of his gaze.

"I was thinking," he called, holding very still.

In her experience a woman had to beware of a man who'd been thinking. "About what?" she asked.

"Maybe you'd like to name the dog."

The suggestion caught her off guard. "You'd really let me choose a name for your dog?"

He didn't set any records closing the barn door, but he ambled toward her, his limp all the more noticeable since it slowed down a man who was so naturally made for strength and speed.

She wasn't a mystical, whimsical woman, or a particularly romantic one. She knew herself inside and out, her limits and goals, her strengths and weaknesses. She was a modern-day woman with a smart mouth, a sore heart and an honest soul. And she honestly didn't know what to do about Wes Stryker.

"A friend of mine gave her dog her middle name, although now that I think of it, her mother had a fit," she said. "You could do that, I suppose. What is your middle name, anyway?"

He grimaced. "You don't want to know."

"Now I have to know."

Resting his hands on his hips, he lifted one shoulder sheepishly. "You'll laugh. Everyone laughs."

"I won't, I promise."

He hesitated a little longer, and then, in a voice so quiet

she had to strain to hear over the crunch his boots made on the crusty snow, he said, "Engelbert."

She had to bite her lip to keep from grinning. "Your parents named you Wesley Engelbert Stryker?"

His nod was accompanied by a sigh. "My mother was a huge fan of Engelbert Humperdinck."

She had to turn around to hide her grin, but she was pretty sure he could hear the smile in her voice as she said, "That dog doesn't really look like an Engelbert."

"Who does?"

Her smile grew. "I'll see what I can do about coming up with something else."

"I would appreciate that."

Neither of them said goodbye, but Jayne glanced toward the house after she'd backed from the driveway. Wes hadn't moved and was watching her from underneath the brim of his worn Stetson. He looked down suddenly and reached into his pocket, pulling out a portable phone.

Before she drove away, she saw him raise the antenna and say something into the mouthpiece. She couldn't see his expression, but his head was tilted slightly, one knee bent, a hand in one pocket. He didn't seem to mind the cold or the fact that he was all alone on Christmas morning. Wesley Engelbert Stryker appeared relaxed and comfortable talking to whoever was on the other end of that phone.

Wesley Engelbert Stryker. Lord, what a name.

What a man.

Chapter Three

The phone rang just as Wes was taking a frozen dinner out of the microwave. It was the third phone call he'd had since talking to Annabell earlier that morning. The kids were excited and nervous and curious, not to mention a little afraid of yet another change in their lives.

He left the dinner on top of the stove. Leaning a hip against the counter, he listened intently to the tiny voice on the other end of the line.

"Yes, Olivia, honey. You'll have your own room... Of course you can bring all your stuff.... Even Snuggles the goose...especially Snuggles the goose.... Uh-huh. And all your pictures of your mommy and daddy.... Yes, you have to bring Logan, too. He's your brother. No, Olivia, you can't—"

There was a screech that put Wes in mind of permanent hearing loss. A scuffle followed, and then a young boy's voice claimed the line. "It's me, Uncle Wes. Logan."

As if there were forty other ten-year-old boys who called him Uncle Wes. "What did you do to your sister?" Wes asked calmly.

"I didn't do anything to her. Well, hardly anything. She's such a baby. Ouch. She pinched me."

"I'm sure she didn't...Logan..."

Olivia screeched again, which made Wes wonder what kind of retaliation Logan had inflicted upon his little sister. "Logan. Logan? Stop bugging your sister and listen to me for a minute... What?... I know... Yeah, I'll teach you to ride your dad's horse. Tell Olivia I'll teach her, too."

The boy did as he was instructed. Olivia stopped crying in the background, and for the moment at least, peace reigned in a tiny two-bedroom house two hundred and twenty miles away.

The next voice he heard was old and as raspy as if she'd just knocked back a shot of whiskey. Annabell hadn't, of course. She hadn't drunk anything stronger than tea since her seventy-fifth birthday. "That," she said, clearly referring to the little skirmish that had just taken place in her living room, "is why I need your help, Wesley. These children pick on each other worse than two roosters in one henhouse."

Wes grinned at the analogy. While the eighty-two-year-old woman talked about aching joints and brittle bones, Wes pictured her in his mind. She was probably sitting in a chair that was older than he was, ankles crossed, her prim-and-proper dress hanging limply on a body that had always been small but had grown gaunt these past several months.

"I know it was my idea to take the kids," she said. "With Kate and Dusty gone, they're all the family I have left, except you, of course. Why, remember that time you and Dusty showed up on my doorstep three sheets to the wind?"

"Could you narrow it down a little, Annabell?" he asked. "When Dusty and I first hit the rodeo circuit we used to show up on your doorstep three sheets to the wind every time we passed through Sioux Falls."

She practically cackled. "Those were the days, weren't they?"

Her cough didn't fool Wes into believing that the sudden thickness in her voice was anything other than tears. Being the tough old bird she was, Annabell recovered and said, "Those were the days then, and these are the days now. I spoke to a judge friend of mine, discreetly, mind you. He says he doesn't foresee any major problems or obstacles with placing the children with you. It would be easier if you were blood related, but you are their godfather, after all. You're going to have to go through the proper channels, though."

"What channels?" Wes asked, uncrossing his ankles and standing up straighter.

"You'll have to show the system that you can provide for Logan and Olivia, that you have a suitable place for them to live, that sort of thing. There'll be some paperwork involved, but isn't there always? Stanley said that in a perfect world the state would prefer to place children in two-parent homes. I'm telling you, if I were twenty years younger, I'd move out there and marry you myself."

Wes smiled to himself. If Annabell Malone were twenty years younger, she would still be twenty-seven years older than he was.

"I know there's been a noted lack of women in Jasper Gulch these past several years," Annabell said. "But can you think of a woman who stirs your juices, so to speak, and who might take to these two corkers?"

Wes's gaze shifted to the window over the sink and beyond, to the road that led to town. As a matter of fact, he couldn't stop thinking about a woman who stirred his juices, so to speak. A woman who knew how to swear and sputter, and who seemed to have an innate ability to see beyond the surface of a scrawny kitten, a mangy dog and maybe even a battered ex-rodeo champion. The woman he was thinking about had lightning-quick reflexes, a lush mouth, a bristly attitude and a body that could keep a man awake at night without even being in the room. Wes happened to like her attitude, and although he knew she *claimed* that she'd sworn off men, all men, she'd driven out to the ranch to help a man in need.

A noise in his ear snagged his attention. "What? Oh, Annabell, of course I was listening."

The kids were at it again, fighting in the background. Poor Annabell muttered that she had to go.

Wes hung up on his end, smiling. No wonder that woman sounded so tired. Some people couldn't stand it when kids argued. He happened to think it was a far sight better than how utterly quiet Logan and Olivia had been in the days immediately following their parents' funerals six months ago. He'd take healthy bickering any day. Those two hellions certainly did their share of that. Kate used to say it was the five-year age difference. Dusty always claimed it was the gender difference. Wes happened to think the kids just plain enjoyed fighting. There were lots of people in the world like that.

Take Jayne Kincaid, for instance.

Heaven help him, that was exactly what he wanted to do.

Six months ago he'd been a footloose rodeo champion. Now, he had a woman to woo, and two children to make a home for. He looked around him with a critical eye, wondering what a social worker would say about the old house he'd inherited along with a staggering amount of back taxes and a ranch that was so rundown it was practically hopeless.

The kitchen, at least, was functional, although not very appealing to the eye. The plumbing was adequate, but the entire place needed repairs, several new windows and a thorough cleaning. According to Annabell's calculations, it would take a little less than a month to process all the paperwork. That didn't leave him a lot of time to spruce up the place, to get the ranch operational and to lure one gun-shy woman into his arms and into his life.

By the time Wes went back to his dinner, a wan shaft of sunlight had filtered into the room. That old sun couldn't shine brightly this time of year no matter how hard it tried. Rather than appearing as a burning ball of fire, it was more like a glittering promise of what was to come.

He ate his dinner in silence, smack-dab in the middle of that shaft of light. Funny thing about that sunbeam. Faint though it might be, it was surprisingly warm. That was because there was more to sunlight than met the eye. Jayne was like that, too, although what met the eye was damned appealing. Something told him she didn't invite many people to explore the deeper layers of her personality, and yet she'd driven out here on Christmas morning, braving ice and snow. She'd helped him to his feet, and then she'd offered her own brand of comfort and empathy over the loss of his best friend. She could be tough when she wanted to be, but Wes had witnessed her softer side. He shifted in his chair. It was interesting what thinking about a woman's soft side could do to a man's body.

He wondered how long she would wait to come back out to the ranch. Offering to let her name the dog had been an inspiration. Although it hadn't been precalculated, it had been brilliant. She would be back. To name the dog, and to see him. Ah, yes, that patch of weak winter sunlight was incredibly bright with promise.

"What do you two think of the name Irving?"

Louetta and Burke both glanced across the counter in the diner where Jayne was fiddling with the sugars and creamers.

"Are you thinking about having a baby?" Louetta asked.

Jayne tilted her head dramatically. "God, no. I'm trying to come up with a name for a dog."

"How about Fido?" Louetta asked.

Jayne shook her head. "No, this has to be a name for a proud dog. A stray."

"I see," Burke said. "How about Champ?"

"No-o-o-o."

"Trusty?" Louetta offered.

"I don't think so."

"Chauncy?"

Jayne and Burke found themselves following Louetta into the kitchen where she immediately started loading breakfast dishes into a shiny new dishwasher. "I've always thought Blue would be a good name for a dog," Louetta said in that quiet way she had.

Jayne shrugged. "I was thinking more along the lines of a less traditional name."

The clattering of silverware stopped momentarily while Louetta tucked a wavy tendril of her light brown hair behind her ear. "Hmm," she said, lithely going back to her task. "That eliminates Bowser and Tramp."

"And Rocky or Spike," Burke added.

Jayne wandered aimlessly from one end of the kitchen to the other. She put a gallon of milk away for something to do. While she had the refrigerator open, she stared at the ham bone she'd wrapped in plastic and the apples and the container of buttermilk she'd picked up at the grocery store earlier. Dogs loved bones, and kittens, milk, and horses, apples, didn't they?

"I considered Oswald and Hercules," she said, closing the door and pacing once again. "But neither of them seems to fit."

"Oswald and Hercules?" Louetta asked.

Shrugging sheepishly, no small feat for Jayne, she said, "It's Wes's dog, and he's very unusual. The dog, I mean."

If Jayne had been watching, she would have seen the look Burke and Louetta exchanged, the lift of his eyebrows as he asked a silent question and the way she gestured for him to leave the two women alone.

"Well," he said, raising his hands over his head in a stretch that was just a little too casual to go unnoticed. "I have patients to see." He kissed his new wife and gave Jayne a brotherly nudge.

Jayne watched him closely, because, newlywed or not, he simply was not a man who was given to casual shrugs or brotherly nudges. Burke pushed through the swinging door leading to the dining room, and ultimately to the front door, calling over his shoulder, "How about Peerpont?"

She rolled her eyes, calling back, "That's almost as bad as Engelbert."

"Engelbert?" Louetta said.

Jayne stopped abruptly. Where had that come from? Luckily Louetta was busy and didn't seem to notice her sudden agitation.

Jayne *was* agitated. She felt antsy, as if she needed to climb out of her skin. Pacing to the side wall and back again, she knew what her problem was. She wasn't accustomed to having so much time on her hands, and she was going stir-crazy.

It was the day after Christmas. She could have spent the next week with her half-brother in Oklahoma City, but he was doing stand-up comedy, and since her divorce, she'd lost the ability to laugh. Her mother had invited her down to California to spend the holidays with her and her latest husband, but Jayne hadn't felt up to defending her hairstyle and her choice of clothes. Her father was on a cruise with his newest girlfriend. At least he'd wised up and no longer married every woman he professed to love.

"Are you chilled?" Louetta asked.

What?

Jayne shook her head and came to her senses. She *had* shivered, but the goose bumps were more like the kind a person got after scraping her fingernail on a chalkboard than those that came from the cold. "Oh, no. I'm just edgy. I think it's time I went back to Seattle."

Louetta was suddenly directly in front of her. "So soon?"

"I've been here two weeks," Jayne reminded her.

"I know, but it's nice having another woman to talk to. I haven't had that since my mother died two years ago. I was hoping you'd stay, rest, recover from the divorce."

"You make my divorce sound like a car accident. It isn't as if I'm coming out of a coma, you know."

Memories of the dream she'd had a few nights ago filtered into her thoughts, causing her body to tingle and her heart to swell as if it was slowly coming back to life. In a strange way, she supposed she did feel as if she were coming out of a coma.

She inhaled sharply and set off in the opposite direction. "I need to keep busy."

Louetta stared at her for several seconds, then quietly said, "If you're looking for something to do, I can always use help in the diner."

"You want *me* to waitress?"

Louetta's smile slipped a notch. "I know my diner doesn't look like much, but waiting tables is honest work, and..."

"Of course it is," Jayne interrupted. "It's just that— Are you sure you want me to do it? I mean, I'm not what most people would call a people person."

A fresh, new smile washed over Louetta's pretty face. "Nonsense. I think you're very sweet. Wes must, too, or he wouldn't want you to choose his dog's name."

Bells sounded in Jayne's head. Lights flared, alarms buzzed, and flags went up. Suddenly she understood what was at the root of her agitation. Choosing a name, even a dog's name, was a very personal undertaking. It created a bond between the person doing the naming and the person who owned the dog.

The thought brought her up short. Good grief, what had she almost done?

The bell jingled in the diner. Peeking through a crack in the door, Louetta said, "It's Cletus McCully. Would you like to start work now or after you've taken those treats out to the Double S?"

Wondering how on earth Louetta could have known what she'd originally planned to do, Jayne shook her head. "I think I'd like to begin right now." Before she did something she would regret, something she'd promised herself she would never do again. Before she grew attached to a man who could ultimately break her heart.

She wasn't going to come.

Wes tested the new window he'd just replaced, sliding it up and down, checking for a good fit and tight seal. He'd kept himself very busy cleaning out the horse stalls and replacing boarded-up windows with panes of glass and re-routing the downspout so rainwater wouldn't run between the back door and the driveway and freeze into a solid pool of ice. He'd put in sixteen-hour days, five days in a row. Jayne hadn't shown up.

He hadn't thought too much of it the first day. When she'd failed to show up on the second, he'd started to get suspicious. It wasn't as if he didn't have plenty to do. He'd been in touch with an attorney in Pierre; the paperwork was on its way. He'd talked to Olivia and Logan every day, so it was possible that Jayne had tried to call but hadn't been able to get through. He doubted she'd tried. And he knew for a fact that she hadn't come anywhere near this old ranch. He'd watched the road, he'd listened for the sound of a car and he'd waited.

She hadn't come.

He told himself he had no reason to be disappointed. He wished he had a stiff drink. Throwing down his hammer, he headed for the shower, telling himself the whole time he was peeling off his clothes that Jayne probably had a perfectly good reason for staying away. Contrary, confounded woman couldn't just make this easy. Why in Sam Hill hadn't she come?

He stepped under the spray of water and licked his lips. Better make that a double.

The Crazy Horse crowd was thin but predictable. There was talk of getting a poker game going, and one or two of the boys suggested firing up the mechanical bull, but so far nobody had done more than grumble and take an occasional sip from the long-necked bottles in front of them.

As usual, Wes spoke when spoken to. Otherwise, he remained quiet, lost in his own thoughts.

"Sure would be nice if the sun would poke through those clouds one of these days," Ben Jacobs grumbled.

"The gloom is depressing the herd," one of the Anderson brothers, Wes thought it was Ned, complained.

"Mine, too," somebody else groused.

Wes picked up his bottle of beer, drinking half of it before placing it back on the table. After that, he lost track of who was saying what.

"The weatherman's predicting more snow."

"Gonna be a long winter."

"At least it ain't raining. What do ya think about those floods down in Texas?"

"Depressing. Downright depressing. But you know what they say. If it ain't locust plagues or bottomed-out beef prices, it's droughts or floods."

"The shortage of women ain't helping."

"Yeah. We could all use a little female companionship."

"I guess we're gonna have to settle for a slice of Louetta's homemade pie."

"I dare you to order it. For crying out loud. I don't even feel welcome in the diner anymore. That new waitress might be easy on the eyes, but she's murder on a man's ears."

Wes's ears perked up, homing in on the present conversation. Somebody new was working at the diner? He could think of only one woman who was both easy on a man's eyes and murder on his ears.

"I don't know what Louetta was thinking, hiring that— that woman," Forest Wilkie declared.

"Why, she told me I eat with my mouth open," Ben Jacobs sputtered.

"Says I oughta think twice about ordering dessert. Can you believe that?" Jed Harley asked, his face turning red from holding in his stomach.

"Wes, where are you going?" Ben asked.

Wes dropped a couple of bills on the table and was halfway to the door before he answered. "I just got my appetite back." Lifting his hat from the hook by the door, he added, "I think I'll mosey on over to the diner and order a bite to eat."

"I wouldn't if I were you," Ben said.

"Me, neither," Forest agreed from his position at the end of the bar. "But if we can't talk you out of it, here, take these."

Wes held out his hand. "Antacid tablets?"

Forest nodded sagely. "Most of us have taken to chewing a couple of them *before* we sit down."

Wes handed the small roll of tablets back to the other man. "Thanks, but that won't be necessary."

Two or three men called out their condolences. DoraLee

Brown, the fifty-something owner of the Crazy Horse, raised a penciled-on eyebrow and said, "Most folks have good reasons for acting the way they do. I know how it feels to have a man do you wrong. Be nice to her, ya hear?"

Wes nodded before strolling out of the saloon and across the street. He paused just inside the diner's front door and glanced around. The place was unnaturally deserted for six o'clock on a Thursday. He took a seat at a nearby table. Within seconds the kitchen door swung open, and his eyes met Jayne's. Her slight hesitation was barely discernible, and as far as he was concerned, very telling.

Man, but she was a sight for sore eyes. Her dark hair looked pleasantly mussed. Her jeans were ordinary enough, but he'd never seen anything like the canary yellow shirt tucked into them. There weren't many people who could wear canary yellow. There weren't many people who would try.

"Evenin', ma'am," he said, his voice very quiet and his gaze very steady.

"Wes." Jayne had known Wes would probably come into the diner sooner or later. She'd told herself that seeing him again would be no big deal, and she cursed the shock running through her at this very moment. Although she kept a tight rein on her expression, she knew what it meant when a man looked at a woman the way he was looking at her, and she understood what could happen when a woman understood what it meant. Oh, no. She was thinking in spirals, warm, shimmery spirals that started in her mind and slowly worked their way lower. And lower. Until she was reacting to feelings instead of thinking at all.

Oh, no, I'm not, she thought, reaching into her apron pocket for her pad and pencil. She'd learned her lesson the hard way, which was pretty much the way she'd learned everything. She didn't have to give in to these shimmery spirals any more than she had to give in to the invitation in Wes's eyes right now.

Eyeing his elbows on the table, she said, "Were you born in a barn, Stryker?"

She would have felt better if he hadn't looked her up and down so thoroughly before saying, "As a matter of fact, I was." Leaving his elbows where they were, he said, "How have you been, Jayne?"

She had to swallow before she could answer. "Not so bad, I guess. How about you?"

Wes hadn't missed that slight hesitation or small, telling shrug. Eyeing her steadily, he said, "I've been keeping myself busy, working up an appetite."

Her chin came up and her shoulders went back like a woman who was preparing to put a man in his place. Wes grinned for the first time in five days. "You wanna bring me a cup of coffee and the special, and maybe something for yourself?"

She stared at him for a full five seconds before sliding the pad and pencil back into her apron pocket. He couldn't tell if she'd decided to postpone the scathing comment indefinitely, or only until after she'd brought him his meal, but she turned without a word and headed for the kitchen.

He heard a few clunks and rattles, a clang of a tray, and another rattle or two. And then the door opened again, and Jayne appeared, his supper balanced precariously on a round tray in a manner that made Wes wonder if this was her first waitressing job.

He barely glanced at the plate she placed in front of him. "What are you doing, Jayne?"

"You said you wanted the special. Tonight it's scalloped potatoes and ham."

"No. I mean what are you doing here?"

She glanced around. "I'm holding down the fort for Louetta."

Removing his hat with one hand, he dropped it into an adjacent chair. He took his time polishing his silverware with his napkin. Fork in hand, he looked around the diner. Although he hadn't spent much time in Jasper Gulch until the past couple of months, he'd been in the diner enough to know its specials. Mesquite steak on Monday, meat loaf on Tuesday, rib eye and baby potatoes on Wednesday, scalloped potatoes with baked ham on Thursdays—Jayne had been right about that—and three-siren chili on Friday. Folks could get a burger or fried chicken every day of the week, and liver and onions on the first Tuesday of every month. The place was more famous for its homemade pies than for its vegetables, but the main course, morning, noon and night, was gossip. Of course, people were required for gossip. Glancing at all the empty tables and booths, he reached for his knife and casually said, "Slow night?"

She nodded. "It's been slow all day. Yesterday was, too, but today is worse."

He speared a steaming chunk of ham, popped it into his mouth, chewed thoughtfully and swallowed before looking at her again. "Think it's possibly something you said?"

For interminable seconds, Jayne could only stare, at a complete and utter loss for something to say. She let out a long, audible breath, but she couldn't name the feeling taking place deep inside her. A strange sound started low in her throat, echoing deep in her chest.

Wes finally glanced up at her again, a sensual glint in his eyes, a cocky smile on his face. "Has anyone ever told you that you have a dirty laugh?"

So that's what that had been. Laughter. Throaty and rusty, but laughter nonetheless. It was completely spontaneous and totally surprising, the first real laughter she'd experienced since she'd grown suspicious of Sherman.

Tension drained out of her so quickly she had to place a steadying hand on the table to keep from sliding to the floor. Still smiling, she studied Wes. She had no idea how a man who was clean shaven and freshly scrubbed could look so disreputable, but he did. Maybe it was the glint in his eyes or the way his sandy-colored eyebrows drew together. Or maybe it was the way he calmly ate his meal, perfectly at ease in an almost empty diner with a woman who was a terrible waitress and who had a shaky, hoarse laugh.

Feeling weak but strangely peaceful, Jayne said, "I guess I'd better quit before I drive my new sister-in-law out of business."

He buttered a roll and casually said, "It would serve her right for choosing Doc Kincaid over me."

What an interesting tidbit of information.

He took a bite of his roll, emptied his mouth and met her gaze. "Don't worry. I'm not heartbroken. Louetta did me a huge favor."

"How did you know I was wondering about that?"

He shrugged. "A man who makes his living riding bucking broncos gets good at reading body language."

She found herself sitting across from him, asking, "Were you very good at reading a horse's body language?"

His wink was predictable, his cocky grin even more so. "Wanna see my trophy?"

It required a conscious effort to keep from taking the bait and telling him what he could do with his "trophy." "Why did you do it, Wes?"

He was silently thoughtful for a moment. "For the thrill, I suppose."

"Of winning?"

He shook his head, shrugged one shoulder. "Winning was the icing. The thrill came from knowing I was going to climb onto the back of an ornery bronco whose life ambition was to buck me off as quickly and ungracefully as possible. If it had been solely a contest between the rider and the horse, the horse would have won every time. But bronco riding is more than that. It's about strength and timing and stamina.''

"And pain?"

He shrugged again. "I suppose something's gotta keep life interesting."

"That's what I need," she said, chin in hand. "Something to do to keep my life interesting. Something other than waiting tables." Realizing what she'd said, she rose suddenly and reached for his empty plate. "Not that there's anything wrong with waiting tables, it's just that— Oh, hell, would you like anything else, Wes? Maybe a slice of pie for dessert?"

He rose, too, his gaze steady on hers. "I'm not much of one for sweets. But you could tell me what name you've come up with for the dog."

"I've decided not to name your dog."

"You're his only hope."

She shook her head the entire time it took her to walk to the kitchen. She heard him push through the swinging door right behind her, but she didn't turn to face him until after she'd reached inside the refrigerator for the items she'd placed there days earlier.

"I'm not anybody's only hope, believe me, but as long as you're here, I have a few things for your animals."

She pushed the carton of buttermilk at him, leaving him little choice but to put his hat on his head and hold out his hand for the carton of milk. "This is for the kittens."

"For Marilyn, Carolyn and Sherilyn."

She held up a plastic bag containing apples. "Cletus McCully told me that horses love apples, so I guess these are for Stomper and Gray, and whatever the other one's name is."

"It's Bunny."

Her eyebrows went up of their own volition. There was

undoubtedly a story behind that one, but Jayne hurriedly placed the cellophane-wrapped bone in his other hand, saying, "And this is for the dog."

He wrapped his large, blunt-tipped, slightly crooked fingers around the ham bone, and quietly said, "And what do you have for me?"

She made the mistake of looking up. Once her gaze met his, she couldn't look away. Her backward step brought her up against the sink. "I don't have anything for you."

His shoulders moved, the items he'd held in his hands clunking to the counter. "That's where you're wrong, Jayne."

And then he was reaching for her, one hand going to her shoulder, the other to the back of her neck, slowly drawing her closer and closer, until his face blurred before her eyes and her stomach took a nosedive to her toes. Still his face drew closer, and she knew. He was going to kiss her. And unless she changed her mind in the next split second, she was going to let him.

Chapter Four

Jayne might have been able to resist the scent of wool and fresh, winter breezes clinging to Wes's skin and clothing, but she couldn't resist the way his gaze raked boldly over her, as if he liked what he saw and simply had to have it. He moved closer very slowly, very surely, until finally his mouth touched hers. She'd expected to be taken by storm, and yet the kiss was little more than a brush of air at first, the sheer dreaminess of it drawing her eyes closed, her lips parting on a sigh.

His mouth moved over hers, his lips firm yet gentle, sensual and persuasive. The laughter she'd experienced a few minutes ago was nothing compared to the weakness steadily seeping into every muscle right now. She sighed again, the kiss growing more intimate, enhanced by her gentle sway toward him, the slight tilt and turn of his head, until their mouths were fully joined. Shivers skittered up the backs of her knees, but inside, she felt incredibly warm.

It had been a long time since a man had kissed her this way, and it brought more than a rush of blood and a flutter of her heart. She'd read somewhere that a woman could tell everything she needed to know about a man in his first kiss. Wes Stryker's kiss was at once gentle and masterful, arousing her fantasies at the same time the rest of her came to life. It was the kiss of a man who could take a woman to incredible heights of passion and yet hold her secrets as safely as Wes was holding her right now. It was a dreamy notion, which was strange because Jayne wasn't normally given to dreaminess.

"Wow."

It took a moment for her to realize that he had spoken, that the kiss had ended, and that she could open her eyes, which she did, only to find him looking at her, his gaze steady, his eyes very, very blue.

"I named her Bunny because she was born on Easter a few years back."

Jayne stared at him, thinking he'd done it again, struck her speechless, sent her heart catapulting into her stomach, and confused her, all at once. Bunny? Easter? Ah. He was talking about the horse. The one whose name he'd mentioned before. Before he'd kissed her. The horse had been born on Easter, and he'd named her Bunny. And Jayne smiled.

"You're crazy, Stryker, do you know that?"

"Maybe. But now do you see why I think you should name the dog?"

She released the lapel of his coat, which was interesting in itself, since she hadn't realized she'd been clutching it, and strolled to the sink where she immediately turned on the tap full blast. "I've had five days to think about it, and I can't name your dog."

Wes stayed where he was, following her every move with his eyes. So, she'd been counting the days, too. "You *can't*," he said with quiet emphasis.

She shook her head.

"Do you have a reason?"

She nodded. "It's too intimate, you know, final. It's like spit handshakes and blood-brother rituals. Once a relationship is consummated in such a manner, there's no turning back."

Her mention of consummation took his libido past the place where the kiss had left off. Damn, it wasn't easy to keep his feet where they were, but he forced himself to hold very still. Her answer told him a lot about the way her mind worked. It told him even more about the way her heart worked.

He took his time picking up the treats she'd given him for the animals. "Know what I think, Jayne?"

Seemingly intent upon her task, she squirted dish soap into the sink, peered at the bubbles forming and squirted in a little more. "I don't even know what I think half the time."

Now that he had himself under control, he took a step toward her. "I think you like me."

She made an unladylike huff, but he thought he saw a smile lurking along the edges of her lips.

"On second thought, I'm sure of it. Come on, admit it," he said quietly, taking another step. "You feel something for me."

"Hold it right there." She held up a sudsy hand in a halting gesture.

He quirked his eyebrows for her benefit, and he had to admit he enjoyed her reaction.

"Don't even think it," she warned. "All right. I'll be honest. I admit that I feel something for all God's creatures, no matter how stupid or belligerent or tall."

"That's another thing you like about me. The fact that I'm tall."

She opened her mouth to speak, closed it and opened it again. "I do not. How tall are you, anyway? Never mind.

I don't know how you manage to come out on top of everything I say, but I'm pretty sure I should have let you freeze to death on Christmas morning."

He felt far from cold or dead. In fact, he felt more alive than he had in a long, long time. "I have an idea." Glancing at the sink behind her, he said, "How long will it take you to close up this place?"

She looked around dazedly, obviously not following the sudden change in topics. "How should I know? I was in advertising back in Seattle. When I finished for the day, I simply locked up, got in my car and drove home." She made a pained sort of sound. "I'll probably make this take as long as possible."

"Why on earth would you do that?"

"I'm not looking forward to going back to Burke and Louetta's place. Oh, don't get me wrong. Burke is a terrific brother, and Louetta is probably the sweetest woman on the planet, but Alex's constant *whys* and *what fors* scare me. I mean, a wrong answer could scar a child for life. And all that open longing between Burke and Louetta makes me uneasy, antsy. Why?"

It was his turn to look at her, a blank expression on his face because he was pretty sure he'd missed the question. "Excuse me?"

"Why were you wondering how long it'll take me to close the diner?"

Oh. "There's something I want to show you."

She shot him an arch look.

Passing up the opportunity to partake in another invigorating argument, he said, "I'll be back around seven."

"I don't think—"

"Sure you do. By the way, I'm six-one. I'll see you at seven."

"I never agreed to—"

The bell jingled when the outer door was opened.

"Wesley Engelbert Stryker, you get—"

It was too late. The door closed before she could formulate the remainder of her reply.

Wes pulled to a stop at the curb in front of a small white house on Elm Street. Like a true skeptic, Jayne peered out the window. "This is really what you wanted to show me?" she asked.

"What did you think I was going to show you?" Wes kept his grin to himself, because he knew exactly what she'd thought he wanted to show her. She had a very readable face...and a very sexy mind. And she wasn't wrong. He would have liked to show her what she was thinking he was going to show her, but he wouldn't.

He cut his truck's engine, turned off the headlights and pushed open his door. By the time he'd rounded the front of his truck, Jayne was standing on the curb, waiting for him. She pulled the lapels of her fire-engine red coat tight together, and didn't resist when he steered her toward the front porch.

"Do you own this house?" she asked while he was busy fumbling in the dark to fit the key in the lock.

"No."

"Then what are you doing with a key?" she asked, from a place directly behind him.

"This is where I always bring a woman when I want to have my way with her."

He expected a scathing comment. He got a deep, sultry laugh a moment before she pushed past him and entered the house. Suddenly he felt the way he used to when he'd landed on his feet instead of on his rear end after a bronco had bucked him off. It was a jarring experience, but not an unenjoyable one.

"It's darling," she said from the middle of the living room. "Whose is it?"

"It belongs to Cletus McCully. You can see it's unoccupied. I thought you might be interested in renting it."

"Ah." She spun away, disappearing around a corner.

Following the sounds of cupboards being opened and a tap being turned on and off, he stopped in the archway between the kitchen and a tiny dining room. Arms crossed, he leaned a hip against the doorjamb and casually said, "The first two women who moved to Jasper Gulch a couple of years back rented this place. It's been empty ever since they got married. Dusty's great-aunt, Annabell Malone, thought she wanted to come out here for a few months. Since she's just like family, I tried to convince her to stay with me, but she wanted to be within walking distance of the diner and the grocery store and church."

"She *thought* she wanted to come out here?"

Wes scooped his cowboy hat off his head and ran a hand through his hair. Jayne hadn't even looked at him and yet she'd picked up on the most significant word he'd uttered. "You do that very well."

She glanced sideways at him. "I do what very well?"

Pushing himself away from the doorway, he ambled into the small room. "You get to the heart of what a man says."

She peered into an old-fashioned refrigerator, her voice slightly muffled as she said, "Men talk, women feel. It's instinctive."

"Men have instincts, too."

"Please. I know all about a man's instincts. They're excuses men use when they do bad things."

Wes waited a moment to speak, carefully measuring his reply. She'd been hurt, and her trust in the male half of the species was very low. She'd admitted that she liked him. If he played his cards right, he believed he had a chance at a lot more than that with her. First, he had to prove his worth. In the process, he hoped to win her trust.

Returning his hat to his head, he assumed a casual stance

and quietly said, "Not all men are unfaithful. And not all men's instincts pertain to sex. Given the chance, some of us can even be trusted."

One of the floorboards creaked beneath Jayne's feet. A memory washed over her, and suddenly she felt the way she had as a child when she'd stood on the end of a diving board, her toes curled over the edge, the only thing keeping her from the clear, inviting water was six terrifying feet of thin air.

"Care to hear a few examples of a decent man's instincts, Jayne?" Wes's voice carried to her ears, a husky baritone that called to mind long, lazy afternoons and mysteries half-hidden in the deep end of a sparkling swimming pool.

She turned, first one shoulder, and then the rest of her, until she faced him across the narrow room. It was almost as if she could feel her toes uncurling, her knees bending, absorbing the slight bounce of that imaginary diving board as she prepared to leave solid land behind and embrace the water. "I suppose I wouldn't mind hearing a few."

He took his time ambling closer, and he took his time speaking. "For one thing, most men know instinctively how far they can drive on a tank of gas. And I think men are born knowing how to fight."

Watching him, she wasn't sure about all men, but she was inclined to believe that men like Wes were born with those instincts. "What else are you men born knowing?"

"Most of us come equipped with an invisible radar system that can detect a woman within a quarter-mile radius."

Although she'd seen enough men's heads turn when a woman entered a room to believe Wes's third point, she had to curl her lip slightly and say, "How helpful for all of you."

Totally unfazed by her sarcasm, he looked her in the eye and said, "As far as I'm concerned—" his voice lowered perceptively ''—the most interesting and best-appreciated instinct a man possesses has to do with timing, with advancing and pausing, and knowing how long to wait to kiss a woman he can't get out of his mind.''

''Best appreciated by the man or the woman?''

''Maybe you should tell me.''

It required a conscious effort on Jayne's part to conquer her reaction to the tilt of his head, the steadiness of his gaze, the sensuality in his voice. She raised her chin slightly and said, ''You were supposed to name only those instincts that don't have to do with sex.''

His eyes were on her lips. ''Honey, kissing is in a category all by itself.'' And he tossed his hat to the floor.

Whoosh.

One second there'd been an imaginary diving board beneath her feet. The next second there was only air, and then Wes's hand captured hers as gently as a wave of blessedly warm water.

He leaned closer and kissed her, once, twice—natural, undemanding kisses that told her quite simply that he was glad to be with her. Simple or not, they started a fire in her. Or maybe they only fed the fire he'd started earlier, when he'd kissed her in the diner's kitchen.

He lifted his face from hers, the old overhead light picking up the highlights in his hair, delineating his cheekbones and jaw, leaving his eyes in shadow.

''Do you think you might be interested in renting this house from Cletus?''

She laughed, because renting this house from Cletus was the last thing she'd been thinking about at that moment. She'd thought she knew what men wanted and what they thought. Wes Stryker put a gaping hole in everything she'd presumed to know about men. He was a study of contrasts, kissing her gently when she was prepared for suddenness, holding her hand when she expected him to take her in his arms.

"What's the matter, Jayne? Cat got your tongue?"

Perhaps the most unexpected of all was the way he surprised her and the way he made her laugh. Until tonight, she hadn't laughed in a long, long time, and here she was, on the verge of laughing with a man who should have had her running for cover.

When she'd arrived in Jasper Gulch nearly three weeks ago, she'd thought it was the last place on the planet she would want to stay. It was cold here, the wind never stopped blowing, and the sky had been gray and overcast for days. And yet she'd started to dream here, and she was learning how to laugh.

"Well?" he asked.

She turned in a complete circle. "I might be interested," she said, running a critical eye over the sparse furnishings in the small but solid old house.

"Could you be a little more vague?"

She rolled her eyes, striding past him on her way to check out the rest of the house. "Sherm used to ask me that, all the time, when in actuality he could have written a book about vague explanations and murky, shadowy half-truths."

"*Sherm* was a good liar, was he?"

She was halfway up the stairs when she looked back at Wes. "Although it goes against my grain to use the words good and liar together, I guess he was both of those things. He had incredible drive and ambition and finesse. He just had this one, aggravating little problem with fidelity."

Wes paused, one foot on the first stair, his hand on the railing. "Kate used to tell Dusty she'd turn him into a gelding if he so much as looked at another woman. He never did, either, except in passing, and that had to do with that radar I mentioned, not real interest."

She turned around, looking at him the entire time it took him to join her at the top of the stairs. "How long were they married?"

"Ten years."

"Do you mean to tell me that Dusty never went out on Kate? Not once? In all the years they were married?"

Wes shook his head. "Not once. In all the years they were married. If he had, you would have heard her yelling and him screaming in pain all the way in Seattle."

Despite the graveness of the topic of their conversation, she smiled at the notion of a woman threatening the things Wes claimed. He followed her down the hallway, standing back while she poked her head inside two small bedrooms, opened a cupboard in the tiny bathroom. "Something tells me," she said, peering inside the medicine cabinet, "that if your friends had split up, they wouldn't have had an amicable divorce."

"Was yours amicable?"

Jayne glanced at her reflection in the wavy mirror over the sink. She'd lost track of time. On a subliminal level, she'd known she was alone with Wes in an unlived-in house, but until that instant, she hadn't really paid attention to how small the rooms were or how late the hour. The house was dark, not so much gloomy as it was shadowy. The blinds at the tiny bathroom window were probably fifty years old, at least, the slats turned up, throwing glimmers of light from the street lamp on the corner onto the ceiling and wall.

She supposed she should have been nervous, or at least cautious. Wes was male, after all, and practically a stranger. He had the rugged look of a cowboy of old, from his hat to his coat to his scuffed cowboy boots. Yet she wasn't afraid. There was just something about him, something primitive yet endearing.

Shrugging, she said, "I suppose you could say our divorce was amicable. I thought our marriage was different from all my father's and my mother's marriages. Who knows, if there had only been that one affair, I might have tried to forgive him. I believed in the vows I took, and I didn't want to follow in my parents' footsteps. But during the course of my ranting and raving and his explaining and trying to cover up, a series of other affairs came tumbling out of the closet. After that, I didn't see any reason to fight."

Wes smoothed a stray lock of hair away from her cheek, carefully tucking it behind her ear. He'd intended the touch to be gentle, but one brush of his finger on her skin, and all his good intentions went up in smoke. Suddenly he wanted his hands all over her.

"It would be a shame," he said huskily. "A woman like you, losing your feistiness, your fight."

The last thing he'd expected her to do was smile. "If you would have seen me in action, and heard all the names I called him, you'd probably side with Sherm."

In a strange, perverse way, Wes wouldn't have minded witnessing Jayne in action. Lord, she would have been a sight to see, dark hair askew, blue eyes flashing, fingers pointing, tearing "Sherm" to shreds with her words, alone.

"Pardon my French," he said, gliding his thumb over the delicate ridge of her ear, skimming it along the smooth line of her jaw, stopping at her chin. "But 'Sherm' was an idiot."

She looked up at him, her eyes wide-open. "That wasn't French."

"I noticed you didn't dispute the idiot part."

Wes knew he was pushing his luck. Judging by the gentle swat she gave his hand, she knew it, too. Something restless stirred inside him. Need flared, searching for an outlet. And yet there was more to this feeling than need. He didn't know what it was, but it was powerful, instinctive, something precious and dangerous and, hell, something damned close to love.

Blood pounded through his temples. When his ears cleared enough to be able to hear, he realized that Jayne was on the other side of the room. Wes wasn't certain what had happened to his concentration, but if this had been the rodeo, he would have been flat on his back on the ground right now. Figuratively, he needed to roll to his side, hop to his feet, get a grip. Most of all he needed to think.

Jayne was talking. In a hazy corner of his brain—hell, most of his brain was hazy—he realized she'd been talking for several minutes, seemingly unaware of his discomfiture.

"Oh, Sherm had a wandering eye, along with the rest of him, but he was a decent man in every other respect. He used to bring me chocolates when I was worried or harried, which was a lot, and a rose the first of every month. We both liked museums, and he had an eye for detail, for antiques. Unfortunately he also had an eye for the ladies. I think he actually felt bad about his infidelity. He didn't try to cheat me out of anything I was entitled to."

Wes strode closer. Whether Jayne realized it or not, they were finished talking about Sherm. If Wes had his way, they were finished talking, period. He stopped directly in front of her. She paused, and he placed his hand on her shoulder, taking the touch he needed. She went perfectly still, then swayed slightly, saying, "We pretty much split our assets fifty-fifty."

"That's nice, Jayne."

His mouth was close to hers now, hovering mere inches away. Her eyes drifted closed, as if she knew the kiss was inevitable. Instead of opening for his kiss, she whispered, "And since neither of us wanted kids, we went our separate ways."

Wes intended to move closer, to kiss her, once and for

all. Something held him perfectly still. What had she said? Something about not wanting kids.

He froze. Whoa. Whoa. Back up. "You don't want kids?" he whispered, his face now a mere inch from hers.

She shook her head. Still, her eyes remained closed.

"How can anybody *not* like kids?"

Her eyes opened. "I didn't say I don't like them. Kids are great. Scary, but great. Some of my best friends used to be children. I'm just not going to have any, that's all."

He lifted his face from hers, but he didn't have the strength to back up, thereby putting a little distance between his chest and her lush breasts that felt soft and plump and—

His heart chugged, desire flaring up, stronger than ever. Before his passion and his need completely overrode his senses, he said, "There are special doctors, you know, drugs, surgeries. Scientists are discovering new cures and procedures all the time."

Aw. Jayne's heart turned over in her chest. Wes's face was taut with need. She could see what it was costing him to hold back. And yet he was trying to comfort her for a medical problem that simply didn't exist. He really was a very nice man.

She reached a hand to his face, spreading it over his lean cheek, down the side of his face, gliding one finger over his lower lip. "I didn't say I *can't* have children. As far as I know, I can. I'm just not going to, that's all."

And then she kissed him, the way he'd kissed her earlier, only differently, for this was a woman kissing a man, and whether he knew it or not, women had instincts, too. She angled her mouth over his, fitting her lips between his, skimming his lower lip with the tip of her tongue, savoring, tantalizing, enjoying, sharing.

Wes came out of his trance the way smoke poured out of an explosion, with vehemence and strength and speed.

Wrapping his arms around her back, he drew her hard against his body. He could practically hear her blood pounding through her. Her lips parted, her mouth opening for him. He lifted her right off her feet, kissing her hard, because he couldn't seem to be able to get enough of her. And then, slowly, he lowered her feet to the floor and loosened his arms around her back.

"Wow." She shrugged. Smiled. "I guess you already said that before."

The room became silent. Even the wind seemed to die down, as if it was waiting in the wings, like the calm before the storm. Wes didn't know what to think, what to say. That kiss had been explosive, more than he'd imagined, and he had a damned good imagination. He had no reason to feel so agitated, so angry. He wanted to kick something. Something very solid and extremely hard.

He needed time to think this through, and he had to remain calm so that they could get to the bottom of her reasons for not wanting children. Once everything was out on the table, he would convince her that she was wrong. That's what he had to do. Remain cool, calm and collected.

He stared directly into her eyes, took a calming breath. She scooted behind him, swiping his hat off the floor and deftly tapping it onto his head. "There you go, cowboy."

Since there was nobody alive who could fit someone else's hat comfortably on another man's head, he pressed it into place and took another calming breath.

"Wes?"

"Hmm?"

"Are you all right?"

"Sure. Why?"

"Good. I appreciate your taking the time to show me this place. I think I'll talk to Cletus McCully about renting it, but no matter what just happened between us, I don't want to lead you on, and as long as I'm being completely honest, I suppose I should thank you for helping me find my laugh again and my ability to dream. I'd like to return the favor, but I just don't know what I could do to repay you. I would appreciate a ride back to Burke's place. If you'd rather not, I can walk.''

Wes couldn't seem to move. He supposed he was in a trance. It was all that unspent desire. It was all that warm, soft woman. Damn, it was her honesty, and her sultry laughter and the way she was talking a mile a minute. And the fact that she didn't want to have children. Ever.

''Don't forget to give that buttermilk to the kittens and the apples to Gray and Stomper and Bunny. Is that really her name? Which reminds me. If you really can't come up with a name for your dog, you could always call him Tyrone. It has to be your choice, in keeping with what I just said, but I think it fits him better than Bogart or Bob, don't you?''

He would never know how he came to be sitting in his truck, the engine running, Jayne sitting right beside him. He couldn't see any lights on in Cletus's house, so he must have turned them off. He hoped he'd locked the door. He *wished* he knew how to ask Jayne how a woman who was as taken with kittens and strays as she was could say she never wanted children.

''Well, there's Burke and Louetta's place.'' She waited until he pulled into the driveway to say, ''Thanks for the lift. 'Night, cowboy.''

Wes couldn't be sure if he replied, but he knew he waited to drive away until after he'd made sure Jayne had made it safely inside Doc Kincaid's house. He fish-tailed at the corner, completed the turn, and gunned the engine, deftly leaving Custer Street behind. He'd cleared the village-limit sign and was headed for the country when he started to swear.

His head was reeling, his thoughts so far out of kilter

that he'd driven five miles before her suggestion regarding his dog entered his mind. Tyrone? Is that what she'd spent five days coming up with? That wasn't a dog's name. A boxer, maybe, or a football player. Maybe even an actor. But not a dog.

It was probably a good thing she didn't want kids. She would probably name a boy Sue.

His headlights lit up the patch of road directly in front of him, illuminating fence posts and trees along the road. The windshield wipers cleared a path for him to see. The radio blared. Wes barely noticed. His mind was occupied with a hundred scrambled thoughts.

He hadn't felt this way about a woman in years. Jayne was perfect for him. She could match his wit—snide comment for snide comment. She could kiss like a dream. Hell, she could even swear. There was only one little problem. She didn't want children.

And Wes Stryker had just petitioned for custody of not one, but two.

By the time he'd pulled the truck between the rotting fence posts lining his own driveway, he'd decided it was probably a good thing he'd discovered this now.

A good thing, hell. If it was so good, why did he feel like starting a fight? Okay, maybe it wasn't the best thing that had ever happened to him. But he wasn't really falling in love with her. In lust with her, maybe, but not in love. And lust was something a man could control. He just had to put her out of his mind.

He'd put women out of his mind before. He could do it again.

Pulling to a stop in front of the barn, he took a deep breath. What was that smell?

He strummed his fingers on the steering wheel and inhaled again, slower this time. It was perfume, a faint yet heavy, musky scent, potent as hell. He swore under his breath and pulled into the barn, breathing through his mouth all the while.

Chapter Five

Wes hauled a stack of rough-sawn boards off the truck. Half lifting, half dragging them through the snow, he made his way to the back side of the barn where he was in the process of mending the last section of fence in the corral. The wind was blowing, and the clouds were trying to spit snow. It wasn't good fence-mending weather, but if he was going to have the ranch operational by summer, he couldn't wait for a better day.

He turned up the collar of his coat, pulled the brim of his hat lower and made the mistake of breathing through his nose. That familiar, musky scent wafted over him again, and he scowled. Putting Jayne Kincaid out of his mind was proving to be easier said than done. It didn't help that her perfume was permanently imbedded in his coat. Worse, he ran into her wherever he went.

She'd been crossing the street when he'd pulled up in front of Ed's barbershop on Monday, and she'd been coming out of the Jasper Gulch clothing store when he'd been going in on Tuesday. What were the chances that she would

have been ordering a cake for some meeting or other when
he'd wandered into the bakery for a loaf of crusty bread
two days later? The clincher had come yesterday when he'd
come face-to-face with her in front of the freezer section
in the grocery store. The little tart had winked, saying,
"Fancy meeting you here."

He'd tried to tell himself she was just being friendly. *He*
felt about as friendly as a rattlesnake. While Jayne appeared
happy and energetic, he felt more and more like chewing
glass with every passing day.

He wondered if she'd talked to Cletus about renting the
house on Elm Street. He wondered if she was giving any
of the other bachelors the time of day.

Wes took a deep breath and swore out loud. He couldn't
get her out of his mind any better than he could get her
scent out of his coat. He'd taken to breathing through his
mouth much of the time. As far as plans went, he'd had
better ones, but it wasn't completely unsuccessful. Every
now and then he managed to keep her out of his thoughts
for longer than, say, ten minutes at a time.

Fitting one of the rough-sawn boards into place, he
reached for another, thinking he had no one to blame but
himself for the predicament he was in. Jayne had been completely honest with him from the start. None of this was
her fault, and he certainly couldn't blame her for the erotic
turn his dreams had taken. Every morning he woke up the
same way, aroused and unsatisfied and very, very frustrated. If he hadn't been so frustrated, he might have appreciated the kaleidoscope of vibrant colors his dreams had
taken on. In his sleep-deprived, agitated state it wasn't easy
to appreciate anything, least of all the hazy memory of ruby
red lips and canary yellow underwear that fit in the palm
of his hand.

Wes found himself staring at his gloved hand, surprised
to find a pair of wire cutters instead of a see-through bra.

His palm itched. *He* itched. He knew what Jayne would say if he were to confront her with the little problem concerning his hankering.

"Scratch the itch and shove the hankering."

If only it were that simple.

He wanted that woman. In the five days since he'd kissed her, that wanting hadn't gone away. He was beginning to wonder if it ever would. He was keeping busy. Hell, it would take months and countless trips to the junkyard to clean up the Double S completely, but at least the fences near the barns and road were mended. The boarded-up windows in the house were fixed, the main rooms partially cleaned. He had a long way to go, but he was making progress.

By the time he'd made another trip to the truck, his stomach was reminding him that he'd worked past lunchtime again. Closing the tailgate, he peered into the distance where rolling, snow-covered hills met with the gray of a cloudy sky. It was Stryker land, and although the snow covered close to two thousand acres of rich prairie grass perfect for grazing, there were no cattle bawling. His father had sold the herd head by head to pay for his booze. It was going to take time and money to get another one started. Just one more frustration to deal with.

Wes's stomach rumbled again. Striding around to the driver's door, he tossed his tools inside the truck and climbed in after them. This, at least, was one kind of hunger he could do something about.

"Are any of you hungry?" Louetta called to the small group of women seated around a table in her diner.

"Not me," Melody Carson said, tucking a strand of chin-length blond hair behind her ear.

"Nor I," Crystal Galloway, the most educated woman in town added.

"No, thanks," Jayne said without looking up from the sketch she'd done of the downtown section of Jasper Gulch.

"Have a seat," Melody called to Louetta. "After all, it isn't every day that a newcomer gets an idea past both the town council and the Ladies Aid Society. Today, history was made in Jasper Gulch, South Dakota."

"Just trying to keep busy," Jayne said as Louetta carried four white cups and a carafe of piping-hot coffee to the table before sinking into a chair next to her.

After taking a sip of coffee, Jayne glanced at the incongruous group of women at the table. Louetta looked like she always did these days, wavy brown hair, soft, gray eyes, glowing skin. Melody Carson had a thin face, striking violet eyes, and a personality twice as big as she was. Prior to the birth of her second son, she'd owned the diner, and rumor had it she'd run it like a captain ran a tight ship. Crystal Galloway spoke slowly, almost lazily. Even her light blond hair waved lazily to her shoulders. And yet there was something about her dry sense of humor and her vast command of the English language that hinted at a past that remained a mystery to the people in Jasper Gulch. Unlike Melody and Louetta, who had been born here, Crystal had moved here a few years ago. She had several degrees, none of which she used, having chosen to work in the doctors' office, a job the Jasper Gulch grapevine insisted didn't even begin to test her abilities.

Jayne had been pleased to discover that she enjoyed the company of these three women. She was also pleased with the way the Ladies Aid Society had taken to her idea for a long-range plan that would keep the hometown girls down on the farm, so to speak. Although Jayne didn't plan to stay in Jasper Gulch indefinitely, she would keep up on the town's status through visits and phone calls with Burke and Louetta.

"You had those women eating out of your hand," Melody exclaimed.

Shrugging, Jayne said, "It's all in the presentation."

Melody cocked an eyebrow skeptically. "I was half expecting Isabell Pruitt to have a conniption fit when you suggested we need more career opportunities here if we want our girls to stay."

"Isabell has been much more acquiescent since she and Miles started seeing each other," Crystal pointed out.

"Would you have ever dreamed, in a million years, that she and Doc would get together?" Melody asked. Without waiting for a reply, Melody exclaimed, "Speaking of dreams. Has anyone else been having strange dreams lately?"

Jayne, Louetta and Crystal exchanged noncommittal shrugs, but it was Crystal, who had training in psychology, who said, "What did you dream about, Melody?"

Melody pushed her hair away from her face and launched into the telling. "I was on top of a burning building with Haley, Brandon and Slade. I was frantically trying to secure the boys to me with a rope when Haley jumped off the roof and started to fly. I kept yelling for her to come back, but she only laughed and swooped up to the clouds. I didn't know how I was going to climb down, when suddenly, holding Brandon in one arm and Slade in the other, I stepped onto a magic carpet which I'd found in the diaper bag. And then Haley and the boys disappeared and I was sitting on a horse I had when I was little. Toots galloped down the road, and there was Clayt, looking at me as if he wanted to do a lot more than just look, if you know what I mean. Suddenly, the oven timer dinged, Slade and Brandon started to cry, and Haley landed on the front porch along with three of her friends, who were all giggling and talking about boys."

Melody's violet eyes were large as she glanced around

the table. "I know she's only eleven, but do you think my dream is trying to prepare me for the day Haley leaves the nest?"

Crystal raised an eyebrow drolly. "I think it means you and Clayt should get a baby-sitter and have a little quality time."

Melody grinned slowly. "I think you might be right. What about you, Crystal? Do you ever have sexy dreams?"

"Who doesn't?"

Melody refilled her coffee cup. "Is that vague talk for yes?"

Crystal shrugged. "I suppose."

"I knew it," Melody exclaimed. "Come on. Out with it."

Crystal shifted in her chair uncomfortably. "Mine is even more disconnected than Melody's. I'm sure none of you want to hear it."

Three women leaned closer, all ears.

Crystal pushed her empty coffee cup toward the center of the table, resting her elbows in its place. "Oh, all right. I was running through a jungle so thick I couldn't see the sun. Vines were pulling at me, dragging me down. Up ahead I heard a girl crying. I tore at the vines, struggling, clawing. Finally I reached her, but when I stared into her face, I couldn't see her features. She ran away, shinning up a tree and into a tree house that looked a lot like the one in *Swiss Family Robinson*. The next thing I knew I was shaking the dean's hand at my college graduation. Suddenly I was following the girl again, still wearing my cap and gown. Only instead of finding her, I found a man wearing a loincloth and nothing else. 'Me ask for woman. You do just fine,' he said."

"Oh, my," Louetta said.

"What happened then?" Melody asked.

Crystal shrugged. "I woke up."

"Ugh!" Jayne exclaimed. "I always wake up when things start getting interesting, too."

Three pairs of eyes turned to Jayne. This time it was Louetta who asked, "You've been dreaming?"

"Recurring dreams are the most telling," Crystal declared.

"Come on," Melody sputtered. "It's your turn."

Since refusing to relay her dream would only make them more suspicious, Jayne smoothed a finger over the rim of her coffee cup and tried to decide which version to tell. "Well," she said, running her other hand through hair that was already attractively mussed. "A shrink would have a field day with this one. When I was a child I had this incredible fear and fascination of the water. In my dream, I'm standing on a diving board, shaking my head at my father who's promising to catch me. I finally work up my courage to jump when three of my stepmothers capture his attention. He floats away on an air mattress surrounded by these women, and the next thing I know, I'm an adult, and the man in the water promising to catch me is my ex-husband. I notice a woman standing directly behind him. He notices her, too, and turns around, forgetting all about me. I'm in the process of inching backward off the diving board when somebody calls my name. I squint into the sun, and discover W—well, a cowboy."

Whew, that had been a close one.

"Anyway," she continued after checking to make sure her new friends hadn't picked up on her near slip of the tongue. "The cowboy is treading water, fully clothed, which I think is strange, and I'm in the process of telling him so when he motions for me to look down. I glance down and discover that I'm naked. My feet seem to be frozen to the diving board. Strangely, it isn't out of fear. The cowboy climbs out of the pool. I'm smiling, since I assume he's going to hand me a towel or his shirt or some-

thing equally gentlemanly, when instead he takes off his
hat and places it on my head.''

"Ooh," Melody whispered. "A man's man. What hap-
pens then?''

"I call him a choice name, raise my chin proudly and
stride toward the locker room. Only he's there. I try another
direction, and another and another, but he's always there,
waiting for me at every turn.''

"Is that when you wake up?'' Melody asked.

Jayne swallowed guiltily, but she nodded, anyway. The
true ending of her dream was X-rated, and, well, some
things were better kept to one's self.

Melody said, "I think we all need to quit eating chili
before bedtime.''

"I think you all need a healthy sex life," Louetta insisted
before blushing prettily.

Jayne might have told her sister-in-law that *that* was easy
for her to say since Louetta was a newlywed, but the bell
over the door jingled and the object of Jayne's dream
strolled into the room.

Wes squinted against the sudden dimness of the diner's
interior, his gaze falling to the dark-haired woman sitting
at a table near the counter. He'd heard voices before he'd
entered the diner. Now the four women looking at him were
as quiet as mice. It occurred to him that women were rarely
this quiet for no reason. Melody Carson winked, Crystal
Galloway turned and sashayed into the next room, and
Louetta smiled before making noises about having a lot to
do and following the other two women.

Suddenly he and Jayne were alone, and his gaze was
traveling over her mussed hair and her full lips, straying to
the patch of smooth-looking skin that disappeared beneath
the vee neckline of a royal blue sweater that appeared to
be made out of ostrich feathers. The woman had strange

taste in clothes. Since the heaviness uncurling low in his body was living proof that he liked what he saw, he decided not to comment.

Ambling closer, he said, "If I had walked in on four men who clammed up that suddenly I'd have said they'd been talking about sex."

Jayne shuffled a few papers and answered without looking up. "I guess men and women aren't so different after all."

His mouth went dry, that telltale heaviness growing stronger.

"Have you noticed," she said, her eyes on the cowboy hat in his hand, "how often we've run into each other lately?"

"Now that you mention it."

It seemed to require a conscious effort on her part to drag her eyes away from his hat, which probably accounted for the fact that she apparently hadn't noticed his wry tone. She shrugged into the coat she'd worn the night he'd met her and said, "It's uncanny, just like in my dreams, but I guess it's just a coincidence, don't you? I'd better run. I'm moving into the house on Elm Street today."

Coincidence? Maybe.

She was moving? Interesting.

She was dreaming about him? *Damn!*

If he didn't do something, and soon, his thoughts were going to give him away. Grinding his teeth, he told himself to think about something else. Shopping lists worked well in these situations. And multiplication tables. *She doesn't want children.* The most sobering thought of all. His mind knew the significance of that fact. If only his body would cooperate and make an effort to care.

After she left the diner, he lowered himself into a chair at a nearby table, wondering what women focused on when they talked about sex. And why had Jayne been staring at his hat?

"Wes?"

He came out of his stupor slowly. Louetta was standing on his left, ready to take his order. "Do you want the usual?"

He took a deep breath, silently cursing the scent wafting to his nostrils, and promptly said, "Yeah, Lou, bring me a cheeseburger. On second thought, make it two. And an order of fries, a side order of coleslaw and a slice of your homemade blueberry pie."

He stretched his feet out in front of him and leaned back in his chair, grimacing slightly at the pull of his jeans.

"I'll bring your dinner out as soon as it's ready," Louetta said, heading for the kitchen.

Wes nodded. He wouldn't leave the diner hungry. At least not for food.

Wes punched another button on the remote control that worked the satellite dish his father had had installed on the side of the house a few years back. After running through another dozen channels, Wes shook his head. As far as he was concerned, he could tune in to two hundred stations and there was still nothing on television.

It was Friday night. He didn't mind sitting home Monday through Thursday, but Friday nights got long and lonely. He pushed another button, watching for a minute or two. Even the rodeo, South Dakota's number-one spectator sport didn't hold his attention. So maybe he couldn't blame his restlessness on what was or wasn't on TV.

He turned the television off, tossed the remote to the sagging couch and strode out to the kitchen. He'd nuked himself a frozen dinner for supper, so at least he wasn't hungry. What he was, was bored. And tired. Ranch work was hard work. It didn't help that he wasn't sleeping well.

It was all those dreams he kept having. More specifically, it was the woman who had the leading role in his dreams.

He opened the refrigerator. Eyeing the meager supply of food, he considered having a beer. On second thought, maybe he should mosey into town and have a cold one at the Crazy Horse. He wondered if Jayne would show up there. While he was at it, he wondered what sort of dreams she'd been having.

He leaned against the counter, ankles crossed, arms folded. He knew what he would have liked to do tonight. But Jayne didn't want children, and since he was going to be responsible for two kids in a matter of weeks, there was no sense pursuing that particular train of thought.

He just couldn't figure her out. She might think she wasn't mother material, but he thought—no, he *knew* differently. Hell, it would take a woman like her to be able to handle the likes of Logan and Olivia. So she was a little gun-shy. Who wouldn't be after what good old Sherm had put her through. Yeah, somebody should sit that woman down and talk a little sense into her. Wes knew the perfect man for the job.

He started to reach for his coat and hat. Catching a glimpse of himself in a wavy mirror near the door, he stopped in his tracks. Since there was no sense showing up on her doorstep smelling like horses and hay, or worse, he turned on his heel and headed for the shower.

His boots and clothes landed on the bathroom floor in a heap. Within seconds, steam was wafting from the shower, hot water sluicing down his body. He soaped a washcloth, scrubbing it over his skin, a plan formulating in his mind. Yes sirree, he would go for a little drive, and since he was in the neighborhood, he would knock on Jayne's door and ask how she was doing, did she like her new place, that sort of thing. And then he would proceed to sit her down and calmly tell her that just because one man had stomped on her foot was no reason to shoot herself in the other one. That would probably raise her hackles, but so be it.

Wes smiled for the first time in days. Somebody had to talk some sense into her. And somebody had to list all the reasons she would be good at mothering. Might as well point out how a sense of humor like hers, along with her tenacity, that streak of tenderness she tried to keep hidden, not to mention her pride and her quick wit were all qualities that good mothers were made of. As far as he was concerned, it took those women with the biggest hearts of all to mother another woman's children.

He ran the soapy washcloth down his torso, his thoughts taking a hazy turn. When he'd convinced her that there was plenty of room in her life for motherhood, he might kiss her.

Hmmm. The thought was appealing. Stimulating. Enjoyable. Arousing.

On second thought, it might be a good idea to just talk to her tonight. He cranked up the cold water. There was a great little honky-tonk bar this side of Pierre. Maybe they could go there tomorrow night, have a drink, do a little dancing. And maybe later they could do a little kissing. But not tonight. Tonight they would talk. Tonight he wouldn't even get close enough to smell her perfume.

Jayne stepped out of the shower humming. She reached for a towel, frowning, the tune she'd been persecuting trailing away. Was somebody knocking on her door?

She listened intently for a moment. Hearing nothing, she shrugged and proceeded to towel dry her hair. The sound came again, louder than before.

Somebody was definitely knocking on her door.

Swiping the towel over the steamed-up mirror, she considered ignoring the interruption. She had the evening all planned. A hot shower, a warm robe and a good book.

Aside from the margarita mix waiting for her in the kitchen, her single life glimmered of sainthood. These days her Friday nights were as exciting as a monk's. When she and Sherm had first been married, they'd gone to dinner every Friday night. The last couple of years, before the house had sold in Seattle, she used to sip restaurant-made margaritas and play gin rummy with Paulette, who had been a friend as well as her housekeeper before Sherm had whisked her off to work for him. Jayne hadn't been bitter. It was just part of the divorce settlement. Okay, maybe she was a little bitter. It seemed loyalty was in short supply these days.

These days, she made do with a good book and store-bought margarita mixes, which was what she planned to do tonight.

The incessant knocking on the door caused her to waver. She wasn't expecting company, but what if it was Burke or Louetta? Or maybe it was that sweet old Cletus McCully with another load of her things that had arrived in a truck and been delivered by mistake to Cletus's ranch instead of the house he owned in town. Or maybe one of the members of the town council or the Ladies Aid Society wanted to talk more about her proposed plan to provide career opportunities to the young women of Jasper Gulch.

When the knock came again, louder, sharper than before, she sputtered under her breath that whoever it was could use a lesson in patience. Before the irritating chump shattered the glass in the window, she wrapped the towel around her hair, donned her leopard-print robe and went tearing down the stairs to give whoever it was a piece of her mind.

She flipped the lock and yanked the door open, sputtering, "All right, already. Take a pill, will you?"

What Wes took was a good, long look.

Jayne's hair was wrapped in a towel, her blue eyes were flashing, the sash of a leopard-print robe tied loosely around her waist, allowing the front to hang open, awarding him a clear view of the inner swells of breasts glistening with moisture.

"Stryker? What are you doing here?"

He slipped through the open door with the same grace and agility he'd used to slip into the chute with a wild horse. When the door was firmly closed, he leaned against it, his eyes on her face, his imagination far ahead of him. "All the lights were on and your car was home, and I was getting worried."

"Worried about me? Whatever for?"

"You don't believe me?"

"Wes, what's gotten into you? I was in the shower. What are you doing here?"

"It's Friday night."

"So?"

He took a deep breath. "Aw, hell." He groaned her name, and without conscious thought he pulled her to him and slipped his arms around her back so fast Jayne gasped.

"Wes, what—"

Her words were cut off by the rush of air leaving her lungs and the low groan that sounded in the very back of Wes's throat. She gasped, the shallow breath she took cut off, the instant his mouth covered hers.

Chapter Six

For a fraction of one instant, Jayne thought of protesting, but the notion was fleeting, and she was warming, her knees going weak, her mouth opening to Wes like a woman a long time denied. It *had* been a long time since a man had kissed her like this, as if she were a fountain of cool spring water and he were dying of thirst. Now that she thought about it, she'd only been kissed like this in her dreams. She wondered if it were possible that she was sleeping, and the man whose hands were kneading her backside and drawing her up against the hard ridge of him was merely a figment of her imagination.

Her dreams *had* been X-rated, but they'd been filled with idyllic, hazy images and lovemaking sessions that had always taken place near water. In her dreams the sky was always muted by a haze of soft clouds, the ground covered in a low-lying mist that swirled and softened like the caress of hands. The portions she'd been able to recall had always seemed real, but they'd been very one-sided and couldn't hold a candle to the way the strong hands that were moving all over her right now were making her feel.

Sweet Mother, the woman in Wes's arms felt like a dream. An extremely erotic dream. His hands tangled in her wet hair, skimming her face, kneading her shoulders, her back, her hips. His heart was pounding like a horse at full gallop. Now that he was actually touching her, he realized that the clothes she wore added an illusion of inches to her body, when in reality, she didn't have any excess weight on her bones. She had curves in all the right places, womanly hips, a soft backside, supple thighs. He could have spent hours on those features alone, but his hands had other ideas, cupping her bottom, moving up, up, circling her waist, skimming the sides of lush, full breasts.

His heart slowed, his fingers inching around to the front of her robe, his palms covering her breasts through the smooth, rich velour. He'd been wrong. This was one place where she had extra. His hands were large, but there was still more than he could hold in his palms. He took his time getting to know the size and shape and feel of her. She arched like a cat in a patch of sunshine. When his thumbs flicked over her nipples, her breathing changed, and she held perfectly still, as if all her attention was trained on what he was doing with his thumb and forefinger.

Her eyelashes fluttered and she moaned softly, and then, reaching between their bodies as if in slow motion, she touched him where he was aching to be touched. He dragged in a ragged breath, and very nearly sank to the floor.

He hadn't expected her to be the type of woman who was an uninterested bystander, and he wasn't disappointed. The woman was more feline than the print of her robe, moving sinuously against him, her mouth doing the most delectable things to his face and lips and neck, her hands skimming, kneading, caressing, cupping.

Easy, he told himself. But he didn't say it to her. A man would have to be crazy to ask a woman to stop doing what

Jayne was doing, and Wes Stryker wasn't crazy, although he was very nearly out of his mind with desire.

"I should be mad at you," she whispered.

"Why?" he rasped, his fingers splaying wide over her soft, supple fanny.

"You interrupted my plans for a quiet Friday night."

"Honey, you're going to have to do better, if you want that to sound like a complaint."

"Oh, I can do better."

What she proceeded to do better made him forget to breathe.

"I almost didn't answer the door," she whispered some time later, the little woman obviously enjoying the complete and utter loss of his sanity.

"I'm glad you did."

"I would probably be better off with my book and my margarita mix."

Something about her statement rankled, bringing him back from the edge. If he'd had a thought left in his brain, he might have been able to figure out what it was. Instead, he found himself saying, "I came here to talk to you. I really didn't plan to pull you into my arms the second I laid eyes on you."

"This comes as a surprise to me, too," she whispered, her lips tickling his neck. "I wasn't expecting to have sex again as long as I live. I don't have protection."

There it was again, a thought on the tip of his mind, an insight into the way her brain worked. He had to think. He couldn't do it with her lips and hands all over him. Capturing her wrists in his hands, he rasped, "I don't have protection, either."

"You don't?" Her voice was husky, her robe open to the waist now.

A brand-new jolt of wanting plowed through him.

Take her now, a voice inside his head demanded. *She*

*wants this as much as you do. You're both adults, you're
both lonely.*

*If you do this, she'll always think of it as a one-night
stand,* another voice cut in. Wes preferred the first voice,
but the second voice persisted. *There's more at stake here
than sex. Think of the children, the future. Think of her.*

His eyes locked on hers. Her pupils were large, her irises
dewy and so soft looking he had to be careful not to fall
right into them. "We can't do this," he whispered, his body
protesting at what he was about to do.

He straightened slightly, putting a few inches between
them. "Don't think I don't want to." He made a sound
only a man could manage to make. "And we will make
love. Make no mistake about that."

Jayne felt as if she were on that diving board again,
teetering precariously close to the edge. It suddenly dawned
on her that Wes was straightening his own clothing, even
while his eyes were trained on her breasts. It was probably
a good thing the blood had drained out of her face. It left
more room for her temper to flare. What had she almost
done?

She spun around, securing the sash at her waist. Never
mind that she'd been spineless two minutes ago, and that
if it hadn't been for the fact that someone had had a shred
of control and good sense, she and Wes would be writhing
in ecstasy right now. She would have preferred that someone to have been her. But since there wasn't much she
could do about it now, she might as well salvage a little of
her pride.

"I had my night all planned, Stryker. The margarita mix
is still on the counter, my book's on the stand next to my
bed. I would have been well into both by now if you hadn't
practically busted through the glass in my front door. Oh,
no, you don't. Stay right where you are. Consider what just
happened between us a momentary lapse. Don't consider

for an instant that there's a snowball's chance in hell of it happening again. Why are you smiling?''

He *was* smiling at her, all teeth, shoulders and ego. The cowboy obviously had more brawn than sense, but my, he was a ruggedly good-looking man. She couldn't believe she was thinking this. Get a grip, she told herself.

"A book and a margarita might do once in a while," he said with far too much confidence. "But I think you and I both know what you really need."

Now that she had her equilibrium back, she pushed her tangled, damp hair away from her face and sent him a killer glare. "I didn't have you pegged as one of those men who actually believe they were created to stir a woman's—"

She stopped, mentally kicking herself.

Wes strolled closer as if he had all the time in the world. Stopping an arm's length away, he calmly said, "Were you going to say *soul?*"

"Puh-lease."

"Juices?"

Jayne clamped her mouth shut, because that was worse, especially since it was accompanied by a wild swirl in her stomach and a tingly sensation slightly lower.

"Why would you say men and women were created, Jayne?"

Something restless and unwelcome stirred inside her. "I haven't got a clue."

"Oh, I think you do."

She bristled. "What? You think men and women were created for sex?"

"Not just sex. Although that's part of it, a fairly big part, I'd say. But I think you know that. Know what else I think?"

"Pray tell."

He almost smiled at her sarcasm, but she noticed it didn't keep him from continuing. "I think Sherm bruised your

dreams, but I don't think he eliminated them completely.
I'm glad.''

Trying her darnedest to keep the tenacious hold she had
on her senses, she said, ''It was nice of you to stop by.
Have a nice life.''

As far as hints went, that one carried the crack and wallop of a baseball bat. Wes chose to ignore it. ''Aren't you
the slightest bit interested to know the real reason I stopped
by tonight?''

''Not in the least.''

''I'll give you a hint. It has to do with dreams.''

She really wished he would stop mentioning dreams.

''I know you have them,'' he continued. ''I do, too.
Wanna hear what I dream about?''

No. Yes. Not really. Maybe. ''Are you talking about the
night-time variety?'' she asked in spite of herself. ''Or
dreams for the future?''

''Take your pick.''

Wes leaned down, scooped his cowboy hat off the floor
and carried it with him to a chair on the far side of the
room. This was it, he thought. This was what he'd come
here to talk about before his carnal instincts had taken over.
This was what he'd rehearsed, and this was how far he'd
intended to stay away from her.

The wind howled outside. Inside, the refrigerator kicked
on, and the furnace rumbled to life in the basement. Otherwise the house was silent until he said, ''If it makes you
feel any better, I rehearsed the entire spiel during the drive
from my place.''

Strangely, it did make Jayne feel better. Only she didn't
want to feel better. She wanted him to leave, so she could
dry her hair and read her novel and drink her margarita and
keep the weak hold she had on her heart.

She'd been around men enough in the thirty-two years
she'd been on the planet to be able to read their body lan-

guage. Unfortunately Wes's body language was telling her he had no intention of leaving any time soon.

"Until six months ago," he said, redistributing his weight to his good leg, "I didn't think much about the future, at least not beyond the next rodeo, the next trophy, the next town. But that's changed."

"Wes, I really don't—"

"Now I see a woman in my future, the ranch in working order—"

"That's nice, Wes, but I—"

"A dog whose name is definitely not Tyrone—"

She smiled grudgingly.

"Horses, cattle, barn cats."

Jayne shook her head slowly, her smile growing. "How are Marilyn, Carolyn and Sherilyn, anyway?"

"They're fine. They loved the buttermilk. All the animals liked their treats. And I see kids in my future. Two, at least. Maybe three or four."

Jayne felt the blood drain out of her face. Up until he'd mentioned children, she'd almost been able to picture herself in his dreams. Suddenly their dreams parted ways. Before this went any further, she had to make him understand.

"That sounds like the all-American dream, Stryker. The all-American family. You're welcome to have a go at it, but I'm afraid it only exists in fairy tales. Believe me. I know. My parents have been married many times. I don't know anybody who marries for keeps anymore. Long-running marriages certainly don't run in my family. Whenever I started to get attached to a new stepparent or brother or sister, the adults got divorced and the new family was torn apart."

"So you learned to distance yourself from adults and children alike. You're hiding a heart of gold, you know. I happen to believe you'd make a wonderful mother."

She held up her hand. "You've got the wrong girl.

Woman. Whatever. Children hate me. I'm not kidding. Strangers' kids cry if I so much as look at them in the mall. And it's not just that. I'm not cut out to be a mother. Alex is still using the swearword he picked up from me. The first thing a psychiatrist asks is what kind of relationship his patient had with his or her mother. *My* mother was terrible at it. Burke's the only one in the entire family who isn't permanently messed up. I won't put a child through what I went through. Wes?''

His gaze climbed from the front of her robe, causing her to wonder if he'd heard a word she'd said.

"This might all make more sense to you if you would try to concentrate,'' she accused.

"Who says I'm not concentrating?''

Her "harrumph'' spoke volumes.

Undeterred, Wes said, "Now that I've told you about my dreams for the future, care to hear about the ones I've been having at night?''

She uttered a very succinct cussword.

He only laughed. Moving extremely fast for a man with a bad knee, he whispered, "Give the lady a cigar. On second thought, I have a better idea.''

And then he kissed her all over again.

An old country-western ballad played over the radio, the volume so low Wes couldn't make out the words. He knew the wind was howling outside, but the doors and windows in this truck were airtight, making the interior as quiet as a carpeted room in a fancy high-rise twenty stories up. Those automakers in Detroit sure knew how to build 'em and move 'em on down the line. He didn't know why he was thinking about Detroit or a room at the top of a fancy high-rise when the place he really wanted to be had two drafty floors back on Elm Street in Jasper Gulch, South Dakota.

He hadn't bothered to warm up his truck before leaving Jayne's place. That last kiss of hers had kept him warm well into his trip home. It was amazing how that woman could swear out of one side of her mouth and kiss out of the other. Amazing and incredible and mind-boggling. In fact, the entire episode had been so unforgettable that he'd been halfway back to his place before he'd realized he'd failed to ask her if she liked honky-tonk bars and line dancing. He grinned in the darkness, pleased to have a reason to call her when he got home.

No matter what she'd said about his concentration, he *had* heard every word she'd uttered. She'd had a crummy childhood. He understood about crummy childhoods. If his mother had lived, things might have been different. But she'd died young, and his father had been an alcoholic. It wasn't as if Sam Stryker had been a mean drunk. Wes couldn't recall his father ever raising his voice or his fist to his only child. He'd kept a roof over their heads, and food on the table. He just hadn't provided anything else. There had been very little in the way of conversation, and no talk of the past or dreams for the future. It had been a lonely way to grow up. Although Jayne's childhood had been riddled with new people, it sounded as lonely as his.

Given her past and her present circumstances, it wasn't really surprising to him that she *thought* she didn't want children. He was going to thoroughly enjoy watching her change her mind. That wasn't all he was going to enjoy. He wondered how long he would have to wait to finish what they'd started tonight. The voices inside his head were warring again. One was telling him to seize the next opportunity. The other one insisted he had to tell Jayne about Logan and Olivia before this relationship went any further. By the time Wes pulled between the new fence posts lining his driveway, he had something much more immediate on his mind.

He opened the barn door, pulled his truck inside, closed the barn tight and hurried into the dark house. It didn't take long to get ready for bed. Reaching for the phone on the nightstand, he dialed Jayne's number. He leaned back against the pillows, one arm over his head, the blankets bunched around his waist as he counted the rings in silent anticipation.

Jayne frowned in consternation at the incessant ringing of the telephone. She'd already read the same page three times. At this rate she would never know what the book was about.

She picked up the phone after the fifth ring. Before she could raise the receiver all the way to her ear, she heard a deep, masculine voice on the other end.

"How's the margarita?"

Her tongue automatically went to her lips, her gaze automatically shifting to the empty glass next to the phone. "Not bad for a mix."

"Wanna try the real thing?"

She wet her lips a second time, for another reason entirely. "I beg your pardon?"

He laughed. And her eyes fluttered closed.

"I was wondering if you would care to accompany me to a little honky-tonk called the Golden Arrow tomorrow night. The place has a small dance floor and a live band. I'm not sure about their margaritas, but the beer is cold, and they serve the best nachos and chili anywhere in the state. Don't tell Lou I said that."

"Your secret's safe with me."

"That's what I like about you. That, and the fact that you don't like to cook any better than I do."

"How do you know I don't like to cook?"

"I ran into you at the freezer section in the grocery store, remember? I'll bet your refrigerator's as empty as mine is."

"Thanks a lot," she sputtered, "I'm already hungry. Now I'll be seeing food in my dreams."

His chuckle carried over the phone lines, straight to her senses. She decided not to mention that he had a dirty laugh, but she had to admit that it was quite gentlemanly of him to refrain from expounding upon her mention of dreams. Still, she felt compelled to try one more time to warn him off.

"I think you'd be better off if you don't get tangled up with me, Wes."

"Tangled, you say? I just had an interesting mental picture. Want me to describe it?"

"And to think that barely a minute ago I considered you a gentleman."

"Don't let a little bantering fool you, Jayne."

"Is that what you call this?"

"What would you call it?"

The vicinity surrounding Jayne's heart warmed about ten degrees. "The name Stryker doesn't sound like an Irish name to me."

She reveled in the lengthy pause on his end of the phone line as he tried to make sense of her sudden change in topics. Keeping one step ahead of him was fun. Exhilarating. It certainly was challenging.

"My ancestors were all Dutch and German with the exception of a Frenchman or two, why?"

"Oh," she said, yawning. "I was just trying to place the Irish bull that keeps creeping into your conversations."

Wes laughed. God, it felt good. This woman had a body that could have sold anything from cars to clothes to magazines and a mind that was so sharp and witty it made him want to devour her, all of her.

"What do you say, Jayne? Are you game?"

"For?"

"For tasty food and a country-western line dance, what else? I can personally recommend the chicken."

"Chicken?"

"Fried, baked, broiled or blackened. What do you say?"

He could practically hear the wheels turning in her head. She was undoubtedly weighing her hunger pains against the risk of spending time with him. In the end her stomach won out, and she said, "As long as you know where I stand, what could it hurt?"

"Could you try to hold down your enthusiasm?"

The smile in her voice came through loud and clear as she said, "I'll see what I can do. What time?"

"Eight o'clock. On the dot. I won't be late. Oh, and if you have anything red and slinky and low-cut—"

The line went dead before he could finish.

Wes stared at the phone in his hand for a long time, trying to remember the last time a woman had hung up on him. It must have happened once or twice, but surely he'd never had this much fun doing nothing, and he knew for a fact that he'd never smiled until his face hurt. Until now.

He turned off the light and settled back into his pillows, staring out the window. The moon, not quite full tonight, was milky white in a black sky riddled with thousands of stars barely bigger than silver pin dots. He'd slept beneath that same sky countless times, but this was the first time in a while the sky had been clear and the stars and moon visible.

The weather channel was predicting sunshine for tomorrow. Wes had never been much of a fan of weathermen, preferring to look out the window and read the signs himself, but he'd happened upon one when he'd been surfing through channels earlier.

He thought of Jayne and fried chicken and a crowded dance floor. Oh, what a difference a day could make. Something told him that sunny or not, tomorrow was going to be a day to remember.

The phone jangled. Wes reached out a hand, the mattress shifting beneath his weight. Already grinning, he brought the receiver to his ear. "Frankly, Jayne, I'm a little surprised it took you this long to come up with the perfect comeback."

The smile slipped from his face.

"Yes. This is Wes Stryker."

He listened intently.

"How serious?"

Worry etched a line between his eyes, and he nodded, even though there was no one to see.

"Okay.... Yes.... Of course.... I'll be there as soon as I can."

He dropped the phone into its cradle, swung his feet over the side of the bed and reached for his clothes.

Was that a truck Jayne heard?

Lifting the curtain, she peered out the front window. The porch light was on. Together with the street lamp on the corner, the bulb illuminated the snow-covered front lawn, the spindly elm trees for which the street was named, the house across the street and her own empty driveway where Wes's truck most definitely was *not* parked.

She let the curtain fall back into place and tried to decide what to do. The book she'd started last night was open on the coffee table, right next to a crossword puzzle and an empty plate that had contained the sandwich she'd fixed herself half an hour ago.

A passing car drew her to the window again. When it turned the corner, she turned, too, her temper climbing another notch. If she kept this up, her temper was going to go through the roof.

She hadn't been too concerned the first eighteen times

she'd checked the driveway for Wes's truck. A man who could kiss and turn a phrase the way he did was bound to have a few character flaws. Besides, she'd been known to be fashionably late, herself. But an hour and a half late?

She picked up the phone only to drop it in its cradle as if it was on fire. It was time to face the facts. He wasn't late. He wasn't coming. She smelled a rat.

That louse. He'd kissed her. And touched her. And then he'd made a date with her. And then that no-good, no-account, lying, ex-rodeo rider had stood her up. Fuming, she called him another eighty or ninety names. When she'd finished, she started in on herself. She was a fool. An idiot. Worse, she was a weakling. Hadn't she told herself less than a month ago that she wasn't going to sit around waiting for some man, any man, to show up when he said he would?

Wes had probably saved her a lot of trouble and even more grief. She should thank him for opening her eyes. She spun around in the kitchen doorway. *Thank him, my eye.* She wanted to throttle him. He was a man, after all. And men were notorious for letting women down one way or another. Sometimes even the best of men, men like Wes, had no brains at all.

Jayne stopped cold. When had she begun thinking of Wes as the best of men?

He wasn't the best of men. He wasn't the best of anything. So he'd made her laugh once or twice. And he'd shown up in her dreams. She hadn't asked for his participation in either event. And she certainly didn't owe him anything. It wasn't as if there was anything between them. At least nothing lasting, certainly nothing permanent.

Her dreams had been about sex. And that's all that was between them. Actually, all that was between them was a yearning for sex. Sexual attraction. An instinctive drive that caused people to do instinctive, mindless things. Things that made a woman's breasts tingle and her blood do a slow, dreamy dance through her body. Sexual attraction, with all its shimmery layers and hazy notions made women yearn for commitment. Coincidentally, not to mention perversely, wasn't it sexual attraction that had caused Sherm to cheat? It was that bothersome little itch, that annoying little hankering that some women and a lot of men couldn't seem to control.

She could control it. Obviously so could Wesley *Engelbert* Stryker. She wrinkled her nose. Not only did the man have a weird name, he obviously couldn't be trusted. He sure as hell was more than fashionably late.

She stomped to the stairs, spun around, and grabbed her book, only to head for the stairs again, half sorry that all the racket she was making was wasted on herself. After switching off the lights, she forced herself to slow down and think. For crying out loud. It was only nine-thirty. It was too early to go to bed.

Says who?

She was a single, independent woman who could do anything she wanted to do. Right now she was going to bed.

She unfastened her jeans and peeled off the Western shirt she'd purchased at the Jasper Gulch clothing store that very afternoon especially for tonight. Calling herself another dozen names, she kicked the clothes out of the way, donned a slinky nightgown and crawled into bed, taking her novel with her.

She opened the book with more force than was necessary and focused on the first line in the third chapter. She sighed. There was one thing to be said for the single life. She sure was catching up on her beauty rest.

Jayne woke up early the next morning, the book she had yet to start to enjoy opened so far the spine had broken. The blankets on her bed were pulled out and tangled. Be-

tween the boxes she hadn't quite finished unpacking and
the clothes she'd left lying on a heap and the bedclothes
that were half on, half off the bed, the room looked as if a
fight had taken place here last night. Poking her bare feet
underneath a corner of one blanket, Jayne realized that in
a sense, it had. At least in the dream she'd had.

The images replaying through her mind explained the
chaotic appearance of her bed. She looked at her hand,
flexing her fingers. She distinctly remembered her fist coming into contact with one no-good, lying cowboy's jaw. At
least it had in her dream.

By the time she was halfway through her second cup of
coffee, the sky was no longer black. She couldn't say the
same for her mood. She still felt like giving Wes Stryker a
piece of her mind. Hmm, a piece of her mind...

She spun around, warming to the idea. By the time she'd
made a dozen passes from one end of the house to the other,
she knew what she was going to do.

She stopped in front of her closet, casting a practiced eye
over the belongings that had arrived from Seattle. The last
thing that lying, no-account cowboy had said to her over
the phone had pertained to the color, fit and style of clothing he wanted her to wear on a date he hadn't bothered to
show up for.

The outfit she chose this morning wasn't low-cut or
slinky, but if all went according to plan, Wesley Engelbert
Stryker was going to see red before she was through with
him.

Less agitated now that she had a plan, she donned her
thickest, warmest coat and left the house, locking the door
behind her. The sky was gray—even though it was already
eight o'clock in the morning—and spitting snow when she
pointed her car west. Not about to let a little snow stop her,
she turned on the windshield wipers and concentrated on

the things she was going to say to Wes the second she laid eyes on him.

Oh, she wouldn't actually hit him. She would never hit anybody. That would be overreacting, a culmination of all the hurts and disappointments she'd suffered at the hands of the male half of the species these past—hell, her whole life.

Men! she thought, turning the windshield wipers on high in her efforts to see through the blinding snow. Any male over twenty-one was a human affront to all women. She'd had enough. Wes Stryker had picked the wrong woman to stand up. The louse was going to have to take her wrath like a man.

The wind howled, flinging the heavy snow at her with so much fury she could hardly see a foot in front of her. She interpreted the fact that she found Old Stump Road as an omen not to turn back. Several minutes later she pulled her car into the general vicinity of the driveway as she remembered it, cut the engine and got out.

The wind pierced through her clothes before she'd taken two steps. Undeterred, she stomped the rest of the way to the back steps and pounded on the door the way Wes had pounded on hers a few nights ago. She kept her eyes trained on the window, gearing up to speak her mind. As soon as she'd given him a piece of it, she would head back to town.

The door burst open without warning. "Jayne, what the hell are you doing here? Are you stark-raving crazy? What were you thinking?"

Jayne gasped. Wait just a stinking minute. *She* was the one who was angry. And *she* was the one who was going to give him a piece of her mind. Before she could open her mouth, he yanked her unceremoniously inside and slammed the door behind her.

"I can't believe you got here. How did you get here, anyway?"

"I drove."

"In that storm?"

She pulled her arm out of his grasp. "You know what they say. Neither rain nor sleet nor driving snow."

"That pertains to mail carriers." His nostrils practically flared. He really was angry. Tough. She was angry, too.

"It also fits a woman scorned."

"A woman scorned… Oh, God, our date."

"That's it?" she sputtered, a snowflake melting and gliding down her cheek. "That's the best you could come up with? Inviting me to dinner simply slipped your mind, is that it?"

"Something came up."

She shivered. "Spare me the details, Stryker. I don't even want to know if she's a blonde or a redhead."

Wes's silence drew her gaze. His hair was uncombed, his face unshaven, his eyes puffy. "Actually," he said quietly, "they both have brown hair."

"They both have—" She clamped her mouth shut and tried to clamp her mind shut to the probable cause of his obvious fatigue. Leave it to him to act out his kinky dreams.

"Where are you going?"

"I'm leaving," she declared, turning her back on him.

"You'll never make it back to town in this storm."

"Watch me."

"I mean it, Jayne. We're in the middle of a blizzard out here. Don't you listen to the weatherman?"

"No, I don't."

"Why the hell not?"

"Because it's pathetic the way the media tries to turn the weather into big news. It's just the weather, for cripes sakes!"

She stormed toward the door. A movement out of the corner of her eye halted her forward motion. She turned slowly, fully expecting to find a scantily clad woman—or two—in the kitchen. Nothing could have prepared her for the sight of the two children who were staring at her, eyes round, bodies clothed in flannel pajamas, mouths full of cold cereal.

"Who are they?" she whispered.

"This is Logan and Olivia." Wes moved past her, joining the children in the kitchen.

"Logan and Olivia?"

The children both nodded, but it was Wes who answered. "Dusty and Kate's kids."

"Dusty and Kate's kids?" Was she a parrot?

Placing a steadying hand on each of their narrow shoulders, Wes nodded. "From now on, Logan and Olivia are mine, too. Right, kids?"

Chapter Seven

Outwardly Jayne held perfectly still. Inside, her blood seemed to run in one direction while her thoughts raced in another.

What did Wes mean those two kids were his? How could they be Kate and Dusty's kids *and* Wes's? Suddenly Jayne remembered Wes telling her that Kate and Dusty had died. They'd been his best friends. And now, these two orphaned children were his.

His.

She felt like a deer trapped in the glare of headlights. She knew she should run, but she was frozen, uncertain which way to go. On the one hand she didn't want to make any sudden moves, thereby frightening the children. On the other hand, she had to get out of there before the force that was barreling down on her sent her flying.

She'd driven out here to give Wes a piece of her mind. In light of the obvious reason he hadn't shown up for their date, the fight drained out of her.

She swallowed. Taking three jerky steps toward the

brown-haired waifs who were watching her warily, she did her best to smile.

Never Let 'Em See You Sweat had been a big ad campaign several years back for a leading antiperspirant company. Jayne was hoping to apply the same strategy to the children.

"Hi," she said. "My name's Jayne. Let me guess which of you is Logan and which is Olivia."

Both kids glanced up at Wes and then back at her. Logan, who appeared to be nine or ten, rolled his eyes and stared at her as if she had cooties. Olivia started to cry with her mouth full.

See? Jayne thought, glaring at Wes. *I told you kids cry if I so much as look at them wrong.*

Looking exhausted and exasperated, Wes picked Olivia up. "I want Snuggles," the girl mumbled.

"Snuggles?" Jayne asked.

Logan rolled his eyes again. This time his ire was directed at his little sister. "It's her stupid stuffed goose."

"He's not, either, stupid. You're stupid."

"Am not."

"Are so."

"You're a baby, and Annabell says not to talk with your mouth full."

Jayne's heart went out to the little girl. It was easy to see why she was frustrated. She had perfectly good reasons without even counting the fact that she'd been orphaned and uprooted. She was engaged in battle with a boy who had four or five years on her and a lot more experience in verbal combat.

Taking another step closer, Jayne said, "Who's Annabell?"

Wes patted Olivia on the back, obviously relieved when the child relaxed and resumed chewing with her mouth closed. "Annabell Malone is Dusty's great-aunt. She's a feisty old gal, and she's been caring for Logan and Olivia for the past six months.''

"Where is she now?" Jayne asked.

"In the hospital," Olivia declared.

"She fell asleep watching 'Jeopardy' a coupl'a nights ago," Logan said importantly. "Me an' 'Livia couldn't wake her up."

"Logan called 911," Olivia said expressively. "And the 'thorities called Uncle Wes."

Logan nodded and started to smile at his little sister, but wound up sticking his tongue out at her instead. Of course, Olivia had stuck hers out at him first and was now grinning because in the battle of sibling rivalry, she had just evened the score. For now.

Wes settled the girl back on her chair, kissed her on the top of her head and told both kids to finish their cereal. Jayne thought his voice sounded as tired as he looked. But then his gaze found hers, and his fatigue was replaced with a simmering warmth that was even more dangerous to Jayne's peace of mind.

"Wes? Could I talk to you in the living room?"

Wes nodded. Turning to the kids, he said, "I'll be right back."

Logan said, "Can we call Annabell when you're done?"

When Wes nodded again, Olivia said, "You promised to keep looking for Snuggles."

"I'll find him." He followed the statement up with a heartfelt sigh.

Jayne preceded Wes into the living room. When they were safely out of the children's hearing range, he ran a hand through his hair and said, "I'm sorry about last night. Annabell suffered a mild stroke Friday evening, and well, everything's been a little out of kilter ever since. I'd already set things in motion to take the kids. Annabell's stroke speeded up the process by a few weeks."

"Is she going to be all right?" Jayne asked.

Wes nodded. "Her speech is a little slurred, and her right leg is weak, but she's stable. I knew she was going to make it when she started barking orders for me to take the kids and head back here before the storm they'd been predicting hit. I swear that woman worships the weather channel the way ancient civilizations worshipped active volcanos. I packed all the kids' stuff, piled it in the back of my truck and started for home. Logan and Olivia weren't too bad the first fifteen miles. After that, she screeched if he so much as touched her, and he yelled bloody murder every time her foot went over the imaginary line he'd drawn on the seat. We arrived back here in the wee hours of the morning. Exhausted."

"Do you think you left the stuffed goose behind?"

Wes shook his head, silently amazed at the way Jayne had picked that particular element out of the rest of the gibberish he'd passed off as conversation. If he'd been wearing his spurs, he would have kicked himself. He wanted Jayne to *like* the kids, but had wound up expounding upon their annoying little tendency to bicker. Bicker, hell, most of the time it was World War III with those two. Rather than blowing him to smithereens with the ammunition he'd given her, Jayne had asked about the stuffed animal that meant the world to a five-year-old girl who looked more like her mama every day.

For a minute it was hard for Wes to breathe. Finally he said, "Snuggles has to be here somewhere."

Jayne thought there was something unusual about Wes's voice, but her mind was reeling, her head spinning too much for her to figure out what it was. "Snuggles," she repeated, skewing her mouth to one side. A horse named Bunny, three kittens who could be males for all anybody knew named Marilyn, Carolyn and Sherilyn, and a stuffed goose named Snuggles. Those children were obviously in the right place. She, on the other hand, was way out of her depth.

"Jayne, what are you doing?"

"I've got to get out of here."

"You'll never make it back to town in this storm." He flattened his broad hand with its slightly crooked fingers on the door a few feet higher than hers. "I mean it. They're predicting another twelve inches of snow and drifts four and five feet high or more in places."

The sight awaiting Jayne on the other side of the window attested to his statement. The front corner of her reliable black car with its trusty front-wheel drive was buried beneath a snowdrift. She squinted in her efforts to see beyond the driveway, but it didn't help. There seemed to be nothing separating the sky from the earth, east from west, the snow that was falling from the snow that was blowing from the snow that was already on the ground. She didn't see how she would ever be able to discern the road from the plains. Heaven help her, there had to be something she could do.

She glanced over her shoulder where one end of the kitchen table was visible. "I can't stay out here with you, Stryker. It's just not acceptable."

His silence drew her all the way around. Now that she was facing him, she understood the reason he wasn't speaking. He was staring at her outfit. She'd chosen it to make a statement. Now she realized the clunky-heeled shoes and the ankle-length black knit skirt and the thick, white sweater with its fake fur trim wasn't having the desired effect on him. It was the loosest fitting outfit in her closet, and it covered her from head to foot. Leave it to Wes to completely miss the point she'd been trying to make and ogle her as if he liked what he was seeing. Things just couldn't get any worse.

She hadn't even noticed that the television in the corner

was on until it flashed off, along with the lights, a radio in
the kitchen and a noisy refrigerator.

"What happened?" Jayne whispered, feeling strangely
reverent in the sudden quiet and semidarkness.

"The snow and wind must have snapped a power line
somewhere," Wes answered.

The children appeared in the doorway, eyes round, feet
bare. "Are we gonna die?" Olivia asked.

"Of course we're not gonna die," Logan exclaimed.
"We aren't, are we, Uncle Wes?"

"We're going to be fine," Wes said levelly. "We're
even going to have fun. And we most definitely are not
going to die."

Fun? Jayne thought. There was no way they were going
to have fun if the power was out. She felt shell-shocked.
She was stuck in a drafty house on a desolate road during
a blizzard with no electricity and an ex-rodeo champion
who could make her blood turn warm with just a look and
two orphaned children.

When would she learn that things could always get
worse?

She heard the scrape at the back door, and knew Wes
was on the other side, his arms loaded with firewood. Jayne
opened the door wide enough for him to shoulder his way
through, as she'd done the previous four times, then closed
it before any more precious heat could escape.

"Shh," she whispered, a finger to her lips.

Following the tilt of her head, he glanced into the next
room where Logan and Olivia appeared to be sleeping
soundly beneath a heavy quilt he'd found in a trunk in the
corner. He could see the tip of Olivia's head and one skinny
little arm curled around a doll that didn't look particularly
loved or worse for wear.

"She finally gave up the fight and fell asleep without Snuggles, huh?" Wes asked.

Jayne nodded absently, then strolled to the window, somehow managing to keep from tripping over the blanket she'd wrapped around herself. It was only one o'clock in the afternoon, yet the room was as dark as if the sun had set. *That* he understood. The sun was up there somewhere, but the snow was so thick not a ray of sunlight could filter through. What he didn't understand was Jayne's uncharacteristic skittishness. She'd fidgeted and paced, looked at her watch a thousand times and chewed on her thumbnail. This was a side of her he hadn't seen until now.

"Are you afraid of storms?" he asked quietly, adding a log to the wood stove in the kitchen.

"What?" she asked without looking at him. "Oh. No. Storms don't scare me."

He added more wood to the fireplace in the living room next, the bark crackling when it came into contact with the red-hot coals. "Then relax," he whispered so as not to wake the kids, although if the popping and crackling of the logs didn't disturb them, he doubted his deep voice would.

Jayne didn't appear to be ready to relax.

Deciding a little conversation might be in order, he stacked the remaining logs next to the hearth and slowly rose to his feet. He ambled back into the kitchen, leaned against the counter and casually crossed his ankles and arms. "I'd planned to take that old wood stove out of here when I remodel. Now I think I'll leave it. It sure has come in handy today. You can stop looking out the window. Nothing's changed in the last two minutes."

"Are you sure the roads are completely blocked?"

"I'm sure, Jayne. Don't worry. I picked up food on the way home last night. We won't freeze, and we won't starve before the snowplow comes through."

"When will that be?"

"A day or two, probably. A week at the most."

She straightened suddenly, the faded curtain swishing back into place. "I'm going to be trapped here with you for a day, maybe a week?"

The woman was murder on a man's ego. Letting his arms drop to the counter on either side of him, he said, "Would it be so bad, you and me and a crackling fire?"

For a moment her restlessness subsided and she simply looked at him, woman to man, an old blanket covering that ridiculous outfit she'd shown up in. Nobody out here wore clothes like that. A skirt, even one that nearly brushed her ankles, just wasn't practical attire to wear out in a blizzard. And those shoes. As far as Wes was concerned, there were two kinds of shoes for women. Cowboy boots and pointy-toed, high-heeled numbers. She probably thought that get-up was a turn-off. She obviously didn't realize that the skirt was delineating the shape of her thigh from her knee to her hip right now, or how narrow her ankles looked in those clunky-heeled shoes, or how that fuzzy white sweater followed the shape of her breasts. As nice as she looked in her clothes, he couldn't help fantasizing about how she would look wrapped in that blanket and nothing else.

"What are you looking at, Stryker?"

Since she'd caught him red-handed, he shrugged one shoulder and said, "Nice outfit."

"I chose it with you in mind."

"I've been thinking about you, too."

His twist of her words had been deliberate. He knew it. And she knew it. Strangely, she didn't tell him to drop dead. Wes wanted to understand why. He ambled over to the marred, old table and lowered himself into one of the mismatched chairs.

"Come on, Jayne, you have to admit this is a romantic setting. It's bitter cold outside, but here inside, it's warm and quiet. Just you. And me. And a crackling fire."

Wes could have done without the sound Logan made in his sleep. It drew Jayne's gaze to the next room. "Don't forget the kids."

He hadn't forgotten about the kids, but then, the kids weren't a problem for him. Obviously they were for Jayne. "You don't like Logan and Olivia?"

"What? Oh, no. I mean, yes. They're smart and strong willed, wily and stubborn and loud. As far as I'm concerned, those are good qualities. It's just that I didn't know about them. I mean, if I had I wouldn't have— But I didn't and, well, I shouldn't have come."

Wes hadn't quite followed all of that, but he disagreed with the last portion of her ramblings. He was glad she'd driven out here in the middle of the first blizzard of the season. The thought of what could have happened to her if she hadn't made it all the way made him cringe. But she had made it. As far as he was concerned, it was a stroke of luck and just what he needed to get closer to her.

"Think of it as an adventure."

"An adventure?" she asked.

"Didn't you ever dream you were stranded in a cabin during a blizzard with nothing but a dull ax, a rusty fish hook and a ball of string when you were a kid?"

She was shaking her head when Wes pushed a chair out with his right foot.

"It's never winter in my dreams."

"Really?"

She sank onto the chair. "It's always sunny and warm, and if there's water, it's in a sparkling swimming pool and I'm standing on the diving board, the sun is shining on my hair and shoulders while I breathe in the faint scent of marigolds and chlorine on the hot, muggy air."

"You're on a diving board?"

She nodded, her eyes dreamy, as if she was picturing it in her mind.

"What are you wearing?"

She turned her head slowly to look at him. "What?"

"On this diving board on this hot, muggy afternoon. A low-cut one piece or a skimpy little bikini?"

Jayne's mouth dropped open. She clamped it shut like a puppet she'd seen on television when she was a child. Wes Stryker hadn't set foot beneath a shower in at least twenty-four hours, which was probably how long it had been since he'd used a comb on that four-shades-of-brown hair of his. From the looks of the whisker stubble on his face, it had been even longer since he'd held a razor anywhere near those lean cheeks and that maddeningly angular jaw. He had no business looking so damned attractive or rugged or sexy. And she had no business wanting to press her entire body to his. The man was exhausted. He had problems and responsibilities and two children who watched her warily and steered clear of her. Like all smart children did.

Jayne Kincaid had never been afraid to face facts. And the fact was she was stranded, temporarily, with Wes and two children.

She'd learned a long time ago to make the best of things. She was a survivor. She'd survived her childhood, and she'd survived the ending of her marriage. She would survive this. She would. "Let's talk."

Those sandy blond eyebrows of his rose slightly. "What do you want to talk about?"

"Anything." Before he could do more than slant her a slow, knowing grin, she said, "Except sex or children."

Wes used the time it took him to settle into a more comfortable position on the hard chair to try to think of something to talk about other than sex or Logan and Olivia. His gaze strayed to Jayne's cheek. A few tendrils of her dark hair curled over her jaw, other tresses trailing down her neck. The blanket had slipped down, drawing her sweater with it, exposing several inches of her neck and the delicate little ridge of her collarbone. It wouldn't take much to bury his fingers in the folds of that soft fabric and whisk it over her head. After that—

"Knock it off, Stryker."

Her voice held all the force of a sharp elbow. How could she have known? And how was he going to keep his hands off her?

Meeting her blue-eyed gaze, he said, "I guess you're going to have to do or say something to keep my mind otherwise occupied."

"I thought we were going to talk."

"Talk?"

"Yes. It's where I say something and then you add your thoughts and feelings."

"You want me to talk about my thoughts and feelings?"

"Just your surface thoughts and feelings. And just until the snowplow comes through."

His gaze slid down to her mouth, his voice sliding deeper and deeper as he said, "You want me to talk about my surface thoughts and feelings." Suddenly he didn't have any surface thoughts and feelings, because suddenly all his thoughts and feelings were deep and dark and erotic.

"I'll go first," she said knowingly. "What's your favorite color?"

"Black."

"Sure it is."

"It's black. Honest. It's always been black. My kindergarten teacher marked me down for it. My first horse was black. Black is definitely my favorite color." He eyed the hem of her black skirt where it brushed the edge of one delicate-looking ankle. "Quite a coincidence, isn't it? What's yours?"

"Never mind."

He grinned, because that meant hers was black, too. He

closed his eyes dreamily. It wasn't difficult to picture her in black satin and see-through lace.

"Dammit, Stryker, you're doing it again."

He opened his eyes. She was right. "Okay. What other surface feelings do you want to talk about?"

She skewed her mouth to one side. "What's your favorite season?"

"Fall. Although winter is fast becoming a close second. You like winter, don't you, Jayne? In winter the wind is so cold all a person can think about is getting out of it, of coming inside where there's the glow of a warm fire and a soft rug. In winter the sun goes down at suppertime, and the whole evening stretches in front of you so that there's just an endless night, and a man and a woman, and a crackling fire."

Her eyes were half-closed, her gaze softer, deeper, her lips parted slightly, the lower lip full and pouty and oh, so kissable. Wes leaned closer, and so did she, their gazes locked, their breathing shallow.

"Uncle Wes?"

Jayne and Wes both froze.

"Uncle Wes?" The little girl's voice wavered again from the next room.

"Me an' 'Livia are thirsty, Uncle Wes," a slightly deeper voice called.

"Yeah. And hungry."

Jayne glanced at the two ragamuffin children sitting up sleepily on an old green sofa in the living room. "A crackling fire," she whispered, "an endless night and two hungry children. Which isn't really a problem, because you said you have food, right?"

He was looking at her strangely, as if he didn't understand the change that had come over her. Jayne decided to ignore him. She could do this, she thought. After all, those two hungry children weren't her responsibility. Although they couldn't possibly know it, they were very lucky about that.

"Well," she said, rising to her feet. "What's for dinner?"

"Soup and sandwiches?" Wes answered.

"What kind of soup?"

"Chicken noodle."

"My favorite." She folded the blanket over the back of the chair and went in search of the cans of soup.

She could feel Wes's eyes on her. He could look all he wanted, but Jayne doubted he would be able to figure her out. It was probably just as well. She glanced out the window where the wind was howling and the snow was still coming down. As long as she didn't have to be responsible for anybody under the age of say, twenty-five, she could survive this. After all, it was only until the snowplow came through.

"Is it just me," she asked, "or does it look like the snow is letting up?"

Wes eyed Jayne and then the kids, who were standing next to each other in the doorway in a rare moment of camaraderie, and then the snow that was gathering on the windowsill. If the snow was letting up, his middle name was John.

And his middle name was definitely not John.

As far as he was concerned, that snowstorm had been the closest thing he'd seen to divine intervention in a long, long time. It may not have brought Jayne out to the ranch, but it had stranded her here. It seemed the rest was going to be up to him.

She'd found the soup and was now rummaging through a drawer. "Voilà!" she said when she'd produced a can opener.

Wes continued to watch her closely. Part of what had made him so good at bronco riding was knowing how to read a horse's body language. A skittish horse was only dangerous until it could be calmed. The same went for women. Since there weren't many women who would appreciate the comparison, he kept it to himself.

Why, Jayne? Why are you so skittish? And what will it take to calm you?

Wes rather enjoyed the endless list of possibilities floating through his mind. Was the snow letting up? she'd asked. He hoped not. The longer it snowed, the longer he had to understand what went on in the deepest recesses of her heart, mind and soul.

"Who wants more soup?"

"Not me," Olivia declared.

"I do," Logan said, pushing his bowl closer to the steaming pot sitting in the middle of the table.

"Jayne?" Wes asked, after ladling another healthy portion into the boy's bowl.

She shook her head, but he noticed she didn't glance his way. He'd also noticed that although she'd been nice to Logan and Olivia, she'd left their care in his hands. He didn't have a problem with that. They were *his* kids now, after all. It was just that a lot of women would have jumped in and taken over in a situation like this. For some reason, Jayne hung back, except when it came to talking. She was damned good at that.

"You had Snuggles when you said goodbye to Annabell, right?" she asked Olivia.

Wes ate his own soup, wondering where Jayne was headed with this particular line of questioning. *He'd* been trying to keep Olivia's mind *off* the stuffed goose.

"Uh-huh," Olivia said, nodding. "I know cuz Aun'ie Annabell kissed Snuggles goodbye right after she kissed me."

"Plus," Logan piped, "'Livia had Snuggles in Uncle

Wes's truck. I remember cuz she whupped me in the side of the head with him.''

Wes almost laughed at the way Olivia held perfectly still, her spoon suspended over her bowl. The only things moving were her big brown eyes, which darted from Wes to Logan guiltily.

"Did you stop at any rest areas or gas stations to use the bathroom?" Jayne asked, her gaze now going to Wes.

He pushed his empty bowl away from the edge of the table, his forearms resting in the circle of warmth left over from his supper. Logan snorted derisively. "We stopped seven times. 'Livia can't go more'n twenty minutes without peein'.''

"Can so."

"Can not."

"Can so."

"Can not."

Wes sighed, because this could go on for hours. He was about to interrupt when Jayne said, "It's a girl thing, Logan. Might as well get used to it. Olivia, did you ever take Snuggles into the rest rooms with you?"

She shook her head seriously. "Uncle Wes wouldn't let me, on accounta germs.''

"Then you never took him out of the truck?"

"You took him into the restaurant," Logan pointed out before slurping the soup off his spoon. "You dummy. You prob'ly left him in that booth where we sat."

Wes didn't know whether Olivia would burst into tears or pinch her brother for calling her a dummy. Her eyes grew round. Before she'd decided which road to take, Jayne said, "We don't know that for sure, Logan. And even if she did leave him there, I'm sure your Uncle Wes could go back there once the roads are cleared."

"Would you, Uncle Wes?"

Wes looked helplessly around the table. "I guess I could."

"What if somebody stole Snuggles?" Olivia asked.

"Who'd wanna steal him?"

For some strange reason, Olivia appeared to find her brother's disparaging comment reassuring. "Yeah," she said, her voice gaining volume as she gained confidence. "Nobody else would want him. I'm the only one who loves him."

Logan took it upon himself to explain. "Mama patched him up a coupla times, but there wasn't anything she could do about his floppy head. And 'Livia don't care that he only has one eye. Right, 'Livia?"

Olivia nodded sagely, then took a bite of her sandwich.

"Where is this restaurant?" Jayne asked, as if asking a million questions over a candlelight lunch of soup and sandwiches during a power outage due to a blizzard was the most natural thing in the world.

"Twenty miles this side of Mitchell," Wes answered. He wasn't looking forward to the long drive back there to pick up a dilapidated goose that had probably been tossed in the trash can without a thought.

"Didn't she have Snuggles after we ate, Uncle Wes?" Logan asked.

Wes tried to remember, but he just wasn't sure.

The kids were done eating and were following Jayne's lead, carrying their dishes to the sink. Jayne poked her finger into the snow that was melting in an old enamel kettle on top of the wood stove.

Since the kitchen was the warmest room in the house, Logan claimed half the table for his baseball cards and Olivia set up shop coloring on the other half. Wes was having a hard time taking his eyes off Jayne. She'd asked him countless questions about the trip back here last night. He didn't know why she didn't just let the subject drop.

She wasn't like any other woman he'd ever known. He remembered looking at her hands the first night he'd met her, and thinking that only a woman who didn't do manual labor could have hands so smooth and soft looking. His earlier assumption still held, because even though she'd offered to do the dishes this afternoon, he could tell she wasn't accustomed to the job.

"Hey," Logan said, his brow furrowing as he studied a row of cards. "Where's my Hank Aaron?"

"It's gotta be there," Wes said. "You looked at that baseball card all the way from White Lake to that truck stop just outside of Reliance."

The look of panic that crossed the boy's face faded as quickly as it had appeared. Wes noticed that Jayne was looking sideways at Logan, water slopping over the side of the dish pan and landing on the floor.

"What did you do at that truck stop?" she asked.

"Uncle Wes used the phone to call his neighbor and tell him he didn't hafta feed the horses today on accounta we were coming home," Logan answered.

"Do you think the card fell out when I opened my door?" Wes asked, worried because that particular baseball card was worth a lot of money.

Logan shook his head. "Nope. It couldn't've. I locked it in the glove compartment."

"Why'd you do that?" Wes asked.

The boy picked up another baseball card, his attention straying. "Oh, there was this truck driver with a ponytail and a bushy beard and a silver tooth looking at me weird."

"The doors were locked, Logan," Wes said. "And I was in plain sight all the time."

The boy shrugged one narrow shoulder. "I know. 'Livia was sleepin', so I just locked the most important stuff in the glove box. Just in case."

The boy's eyes grew round. Wes didn't have an inkling as to the reason.

"Wes," Jayne said, drawing his gaze. "Have you opened the glove box since you've been back?"

He was all set to shake his head when Jayne continued. "I think it was very considerate of Logan to put his and Olivia's most prized possessions inside, don't you? It might be a good idea if you took a look in that glove compartment now."

"Now?" he grumbled, peering out at the raging blizzard.

Jayne gestured to Olivia, and then to the peg where he hung his hat and coat. Wes sputtered under his breath, and headed for the door.

"Oh, Uncle Wes, thank you, thank you, thank you. You saved my life! Mine and Snuggles." Olivia skipped around the room looking very petite and feminine despite the faded overalls and plain navy shirt she wore underneath. Her straight, fine hair was a mess and she had a grape juice smile. She'd never looked happier, the object of her radiant glow a very bedraggled stuffed goose that was tucked under one arm.

Wes didn't know how Jayne could have possibly pieced that whole scenario together, but lo and behold, she'd been right. He'd donned his coat and cowboy hat and trudged out to the barn through hip-high snow drifts. He'd had to do some shoveling to get the barn door open. The rest had been easy. With a push of a button and the turn of a lock, the glove compartment had opened, and two baseball cards and one sorry-looking stuffed goose had greeted him.

He'd taken all three with him back into the house. Although his knee ached from the cold and the exertion, Olivia's screech of excitement when he'd handed her that silly goose had been worth the discomfort. Logan had been much more subdued when he'd accepted the baseball cards from his uncle's fingers. The fact that the boy had been frightened enough to take matters into his own hands back at that truck stop reminded Wes that Logan was only ten years old. He talked a big talk, but he was still a kid who'd lost both his parents six months ago and had almost lost his great-aunt two days ago and had been uprooted again.

It was going to take time, but Wes swore he would do his best by these two kids. That, however, wasn't what was causing his heart to feel two sizes too large for his chest.

Jayne was responsible for that. He couldn't even begin to fathom the way her mind worked. She'd told him she'd been in advertising. Wes had a feeling she'd been very good at what she'd done. Something told him she would be good at whatever she did. Detective work came to mind.

She'd finished the dishes a while ago, and was peering out the window. Wes was sitting at the table, amazed and slightly shaken, the fire dwindling in the wood stove, Logan and Olivia arguing, desire uncurling low in his belly. Nothing about the past hour should have been lust arousing, yet his desire for this woman had never been stronger. The closer he came to knowing her, the closer he came to loving her, and the more certain he was that, sooner or later, he was going to have her.

How could she even *think* children didn't like her? Logan and Olivia didn't even like each other half the time, and they accepted Jayne just the way she was. One of these days she was going to realize that she had all the qualities that came naturally to good mothers everywhere. Wes was so damn glad she'd gotten snowed in here. Otherwise he might never have glimpsed this side of her personality. Certainly the close quarters were going to come in handy in his efforts to show Jayne the difference between what she saw in herself and what he saw. As far as he was concerned, it could keep snowing for a week.

"Get your stupid crayons off my side of the table."

"They're not on your side. They're on my side. And they're not stupid. You're stupid."

"Am not."

"Are so."

Wes tried to remember how Kate and Dusty had handled arguments such as these. "Logan, Olivia," he said sternly.

"Listen," Jayne said with so much wonder in her voice everyone else looked across the room at her. "Do you hear that?"

"I don't hear nothin'," Logan grumbled.

"Me, neither."

"That's what I mean," Jayne said. "It's quiet. There's no wind. And look, it's stopped snowing."

Chapter Eight

The blizzard was over. Finished. Kaput.

The wind had stopped blowing, and the sky, although not clear, was more blue-gray than white. So much for Wes's fervent wish that it would last all week.

"Do you think it's possible that the snowplow will come through today?" Jayne asked.

Wes bit back an oath. "Maybe if you called the county and said pretty-please."

From the corner of his eye, he saw Jayne's head swing up as she turned around. Olivia and Logan were looking at him, too, as if Jayne wasn't the only one who thought his sarcastic remark was a tad unusual. Maybe his huffiness had come out of the blue, but dammit, what man wouldn't be ticked off to discover that while he'd been sitting there falling in love, the woman he'd been falling in love with was trying to figure out how long before she could escape his presence?

Stillness settled over him. *Was* he falling in love? He ran his hand over his eyes, and down his face. If this was love, it sure as hell was nothing like he'd expected. Wasn't love supposed to make a person swoon and soar? Since when did it cut a man off at the knees? He'd always assumed the revelation would be accompanied by the strumming of a harp, the twitter of birdsong and the flutter of angels' wings. That was the way musicians and songwriters portrayed it. Wes couldn't recall ever hearing about someone on the brink of falling in love who felt as if he wanted to grab his intended by the arm, haul her up against him and tell her to go ahead and make something of it.

He pushed a hand through his hair. He could have used a hot shower, preferably not alone. The notion kicked his imagination into overdrive. Two bodies slick with soap and hot water, an enclosed space, kisses mingling with steam and sighs and groans of pleasure.

He shoved his chair out with so much force it slammed against the wall. "I have to feed the animals." Reaching for his coat, he added, "If you wouldn't mind watching the—"

His voice trailed away at the sight of Jayne pulling on her coat on the other side of the room. When his silence failed to draw her attention, he said, "What the hell are you doing?"

She'd opened the refrigerator, which Wes had stocked with a pan of packed snow to help keep things cold. Holding up a slice of leftover steak he'd charred a couple of days ago, she glanced at him over the refrigerator door. "I thought I'd give Tyrone a treat."

"Who's Tyrone, Uncle Wes?"

Dazedly, Wes glanced at Olivia. "What? Oh, I think Jayne's talking about the dog."

"We have a dog?" Logan cut in. "Where is he?"

"In the barn."

"Cool. Hurry, 'Livia. Let's go see him."

Wes ignored the kids, who were suddenly scrambling to

locate their boots and gloves. All his attention was trained on Jayne, who was now busy stuffing apples, for the horses, no doubt, into her pockets.

"You want to trudge through the snow in that skirt and those shoes?"

She looked down at her outfit. "You have a point."

Wes thought this was more like it. He would just go outside and do the chores. By the time he came back inside Jayne and the kids would have had time to get better acquainted.

"I suppose I'll need to wear something of yours."

Wear something of—

He didn't know what was happening to his concentration, but he thought he'd heard her say she wanted to wear his clothes. Now, he was the first to admit that there wasn't anything sexier than a woman in a man's shirt, the cuffs rolled up, her bare legs sticking out underneath the shirttails, but Jayne wasn't talking about wearing only his shirt. She would need trousers, boots, the whole ensemble.

"I'm over six feet tall."

She looked him up and down. "So you said."

"You can't be much more than five-four." The lift of her eyebrow prompted him to add, "Even rolled up, my jeans would never fit you. And what about boots? You need women's clothes."

"Yes, well," she said, rolling her shoulders and sliding her hands into coat pockets that were bulging with bruised apples and sugar cubes. "I seem to have left my suitcase at home. Guess I'll just have to make do with what I'm wearing. Where are you going?"

He reached a closed door in the living room in a dozen long strides. "If you insist upon going outside I'm going to have to freeze my—" he remembered the kids in the nick of time "—patooty and try to find the trunk with my mother's old clothes in it."

"Your father saved your mother's things all these years?" Jayne called to his back.

He glared at her over his shoulder. "Does it look like my father ever threw anything away?"

He yanked on the door and tromped up the stairs. Jayne turned around and very quietly said, "I wonder what's gotten into him."

Gradually she became aware that Logan was looking at her strangely. She had no idea what the expression in those ten-year-old eyes meant—he was a child, wasn't he? And she'd never been very good with children.

"What's a patooty?" Olivia quipped.

Logan turned his attention to his little sister. "It's a hiney. You know, what Annabell calls beefcakes."

Olivia giggled. "Is Uncle Wes really gonna freeze his, upstairs?"

"Of course not," Logan sputtered. "Tell her, Jayne."

Jayne thought about Wes's, well, nether region. That particular part of his anatomy looked pretty interesting beneath the faded denim of his jeans, and the time she'd smoothed her hands across the muscled curve of that well-shaped backside, hmm...

Would he freeze it upstairs? Feeling warm despite the chill in the air, she said, "Oh, I certainly hope not."

Wes hiked a bag of feed to his shoulder and strode to the gate where he carefully emptied an ample portion into the trough. Coming out here to take care of the animals had turned into a major ordeal. By the time he'd found the trunk of his mother's old clothes, Logan had already gone outside where his whoops of pleasure rang through the still winter air as he'd jumped feet first into the high drifts next to the stoop. Jayne had accepted the clothes without a word and had escaped to the bathroom to change. Wes had been more than a little curious to see how they looked on her, but by the time he'd located Olivia's left boot and had helped her into it along with her coat, hat and a pair of gloves that stubbornly refused to cooperate, Jayne had covered the outfit with her coat.

He might have been a little disappointed, he told himself as he broke a trail out to the barn. He sure as hell wasn't thoroughly ticked off. If it *seemed* that way, it was because the hand pump next to the barn had frozen solid and they'd had to carry melted snow from the house. For a city girl, Jayne had done an admirable job of helping him and Logan haul water through waist-high snow drifts.

Yes, he was disappointed, that's all, not disheartened. So what if the blizzard was over? Jayne was still here, and he still had plenty of time to—

To what? Drag her by her hair to a secluded corner and tear her coat from her body before starting in on the clothes he'd found in that old trunk? The thought held a certain appeal. But there was more to this than the need to satisfy caveman instincts, more at stake than sex. Although, if the kids had been occupied doing something else, someplace else, sex was exactly where he would have liked to begin. Regardless of how or where he began, he needed to court her. There was no reason to feel frustrated. He still had plenty of time to do that, even if the blizzard was over. Finished. Kaput.

He might have had an easier time convincing himself of that if Jayne wasn't at that very moment trudging through snowdrifts in her efforts to reach her car and the car phone she carried with her at all times. He told himself she was just calling her brother to let him know she was all right. That had better be what she was doing. If he heard the whir of a helicopter on a rescue mission, so help him.

He dumped some feed in front of Stomper, swearing under his breath when some landed on the floor. Oh, no, he wasn't thoroughly ticked off, even if Jayne *was* making the situation a damn sight more difficult than it had to be.

Jayne slipped through the side door and pulled it shut as quietly and carefully as possible. Following the same course she'd taken on Christmas morning, she strode through a narrow passageway and past a row of stalls. It was indecision that halted her steps near a loosely constructed wooden door with big, rusty hinges.

She wasn't certain what to blame the sudden chugging of her heart on or the nervousness climbing up her spine. She felt as awkward as a woman wearing somebody else's clothes. Shrugging at the irony, she glanced from the man who was briskly feeding the horses, to the children who were trying to coax the dog to come closer. She didn't know which of them intimidated her more.

She'd almost decided to turn on her heels and head back into the house. The safe, quiet, somewhat warm house. The fifteen-miles-from-town house where she'd already been cooped up with nothing to do for hours on end.

She shouldn't have been so hell-bent on giving Wes a piece of her mind. This was what she got for her impulsive behavior. An angry man who could kiss like a dream and two children who needed someone a lot different from her.

A horse nickered, and Logan's voice drew her attention. "Here, Tyrone. Here, boy."

Jayne happened to glance at Wes, who straightened suddenly, his gaze making a clean sweep of the barn. In that instant he looked more like a gunslinger than an ex-rodeo champion. A very surly, cantankerous gunslinger with a slight limp, a steely expression and a mouth set in a firm, unbending line.

Jayne decided to take her chances on this side of the barn. Being careful not to upset the pitchfork that was leaning against the wall, she strolled to the edge of a pile of straw where Olivia was bent at the waist and Logan was on his knees and both were staring at the dog, who, although not hostile, didn't appear to be in any hurry to make friends.

"He's got old eyes," Olivia said.

"Maybe," Logan replied, "but he's got black lips. And that's a sure sign that he's smart."

Taking the cellophane-wrapped leftover steak from her pocket, Jayne tore off a small piece for the dog, thinking that Olivia had been right about his eyes. They did look old, but the animal's movements were agile and strong as he walked toward her, accepting the gift with all the pomp and circumstance of a newly crowned prince.

"He likes you," Olivia said.

"He likes leftover steak," Jayne countered.

Thumping the wooden floor with his tail, the dog barked once, twice, three times, his eyes on the steak in Jayne's hand.

"I told you he was smart," Logan said.

"Can I feed him?" Olivia asked.

Jayne dropped one chunk of steak into the girl's gloved hand and one into the boy's. Picking up the scent of food, the half-grown kittens slunk a little closer.

"What?" Jayne said to the one closest to her. "You think it's time for your milk?"

Having fed the dog, Olivia turned her attention to the kittens, her sudden lunge no match for a half-grown, half-wild barn cat's agility and speed. All three cats clambered to the top of a tall wall where they stood safely out of Olivia's reach, backs arched, tails straight up like exclamation points.

Olivia took the container of milk from Jayne while Logan continued to gaze at the kittens. "The cat in the middle, the one named Sherilyn, is a boy," Logan said.

Jayne glanced up automatically at the cat in question. A male? She'd been afraid of that.

"How can you tell?" Olivia asked.

Jayne felt ill-equipped to deal with the subject. Since it wasn't her place to explain it to the girl in the first place, she ducked her head and the question. She happened to glance across the barn, her gaze colliding with Wes's. The heat in his expression made her suspect that he was thinking about a subject very closely related to Olivia's question. A zing went through Jayne, as straight as a shot of whiskey right from the bottle. Too bad it was only an imaginary shot. Right about then, she could have used the real thing.

Oblivious to the tension arcing between the grown-ups, Logan sputtered, "I can just tell, all right?"

"But..."

"Never mind."

"I don't wanna never mind."

Paying little attention to the argument that ensued, Jayne watched Wes, who scooped up another forkful of straw and tossed it over the gate without breaking eye contact with her. It was cool inside the barn, but not freezing, the scent of animals and oats and hay heavy on the dust-filled air. The kids were still at it, their voices blending with the nickers of horses and the scrape of a pitchfork.

"So what if he is a boy?" Olivia griped.

"A boy cat can't go through life with a girl's name," Logan insisted. "It'll give him a complex."

Jayne thought she saw one corner of Wes's mouth tip up slightly, as if he was on the verge of a smile. Just like that, his surliness disappeared, only to be replaced by something that was even more dangerous to her peace of mind.

"Daddy named his horse Gray. Let's name the kitten Blackie," Olivia suggested.

"We can't name him Blackie," Logan sputtered.

"Why not?"

"He's not black, for cripes' sake."

"You're not s'posed to swear, and we can so name him Blackie if we want to."

"Cripe ain't swearing, and we aren't naming him Blackie."

By the time Jayne had returned her attention to the kids, her thoughts were as erratic as a summer storm. "What about Tom?" she asked, her voice much more breathless than she would have liked.

Wes lowered the pitchfork to the floor. Suddenly the entire barn was very quiet. The horses stopped chomping their hay and oats, their ears twitching as if straining for another snippet of that soft, sultry voice. Even Logan and Olivia were silent as they looked up at Jayne.

"Tom?" Olivia asked, finally breaking the silence.

When Jayne nodded, Logan skewed his mouth to one side and tilted his head, his hat flopping slightly from the sudden movement. "If he's a boy, he's going to be a tomcat."

"He is?" Olivia asked.

Jayne nodded again.

"Tom's a good name for a tomcat, right, Logan?"

"Darn right."

In that instant, Wes saw a lot of Dusty in Dusty's son. Warmth spread through him at the sight of Logan's cocky grin and the way Olivia twirled to her feet and strode to the wall where the kittens were perched.

"Carolyn, Marilyn and Tom," she said, reminding Wes of a teacher he'd once had. "This is Snuggles."

The kittens kept their distance, but Wes had a feeling it would only be a matter of time before their natural curiosity got the better of them and they checked out the strange-looking stuffed goose Olivia had propped up in the straw next to a saucer of milk. By the time he went back to his task, his thoughts were soaring and his confidence had returned.

Maybe he wouldn't have to club Jayne over the head and drag her by the hair to his cave where he could talk some sense into her. Maybe spending time with Logan and Olivia would be all she needed to bring out her maternal side. Maybe nature would take care of itself.

He pitched more straw into the pen, gradually becoming aware that everyone seemed to be staring at him. He glanced at the horses first. All three were looking at him strangely. They weren't the only ones. Logan and Olivia had stopped arguing and were peering at him through unblinking brown eyes. The dog was watching him, too, as were the kittens, but it was the expression on Jayne's face that held him perfectly still. Her natural haughtiness was still as plain as that charming little nose of hers, but there was a question in the line between her brows, a glimmer of surprise deep in her eyes, and a hazy sensuality in the way she pursed her lips. Wes had a feeling he was going to be thinking about those lips for a long, long time.

"What's the matter?" he called. "Haven't any of you ever heard a man whistle?"

Stomper whinnied and tossed his head, all three horses going back to their oats. Within seconds, the kids turned their attention back to the dog and cats. Jayne was the last to look away. Something intense flared through Wes, but he went back to work, his mellow whistle once again carrying on the cool, dust-laden air.

The first thing Jayne noticed when she came out of the tiny bathroom was Wes's whistle. She almost turned around and ducked back into the relative safety of the useless room.

She hadn't known Wes long, but the times she *had* seen him he'd tended to be a little pushy, a smidge arrogant, a tad, well, grouchy. Those things hadn't put her off in the least. She knew how to handle a man's ornery side. A whistling man was something else entirely.

It had been happening on and off ever since they'd come inside after feeding the animals and shoveling a path from the house to the barn. She'd done her best to stay out of his way while he'd cooked supper, although burned supper would better describe the finished product. Wes had been so busy whistling he hadn't seemed to notice.

The hope she'd been harboring that a snowplow would come through had disappeared along with the setting sun. She was stuck here for the night with a man who watched her guilelessly and two children who fought like cats and dogs.

For the first time in her life, two young children scared her less than one whistling thirty-five-year-old man. Too bad those two children were sound asleep in the next room. Worse, she was going to have to turn in soon, too.

It had been a long time since she'd slept with a man. She spun around. She crossed the room where she stared at her reflection in the window over the kitchen sink and told herself that she and Wes wouldn't really be sleeping together. She gulped. Er, at least not in the sense that they would be taking off their clothes. They would sleep in the same room out of necessity, but really, it wasn't as if her leg would brush against his during the night, or as if she would be able to feel his body heat along her back.

"That sound you make reminds me of the wind after midnight."

She turned around slowly and found Wes leaning in the doorway between the kitchen and living room. "What sound?"

"That sound. Your sigh."

"I don't sigh."

"If you say so."

He smiled, and she bristled. If he started whistling, she was walking back to town.

He didn't whistle, exactly, but he didn't look the least bit ornery, either. He was different tonight. There was no doubt about that. At first she'd tried to blame it on her overactive imagination. She wasn't imagining the depth in his voice right now. And the eyes probing hers weren't a figment of her imagination.

"All right, Stryker. What are you up to?"

"What do you mean?"

She didn't buy his innocent act for a second. "You shaved." She clamped her mouth shut. If it had been physically possible, she would have kicked herself for noticing.

He nodded and strolled closer, and she noticed that he'd combed his hair, too. "There's nothing more itchy than day-old whisker stubble. Sponge baths aren't half as good as showers, but they're better than nothing, aren't they? Are you ready for bed?"

"Don't change the subject."

"What subject?"

"Why are you being so nice?"

"You think I'm nice?"

She called him a choice name, which made his lips twitch as if he wanted to grin.

"You're not yourself," she declared.

"What's different about me?" he asked, taking another step toward her.

She regarded him thoughtfully. "Take the dog, for instance. I thought you said Tyrone wasn't even a dog's name and yet Olivia's called him that a hundred times and you haven't said a word."

"I know when I'm outnumbered."

"Then you're okay with it now?"

He shrugged, ran a hand over his smooth, clean-shaven

face, and met her gaze. "Sometimes it's better to let the little things go and fight for the more important things."

Jayne was pretty sure she didn't like where this conversation was headed.

"Take you, for instance."

Now she was sure of it.

"You have a way with kids, Jayne."

"No I don't."

"That's right," he said. "I forgot about that whole 'kids cry if you look at them wrong in the mall' thing."

"It's not a thing. They really do."

She found herself following him into the living room where he sat on the edge of the hearth, his broad back to the fire. When she took a seat a few feet away from him, he said, "Kids cry in the mall whether you look at them or not. Kate used to complain about parents who dragged their kids along to the mall, strapped them in a stroller so they couldn't move and left them sweating to death in their coats with nothing to see except people's knees."

He turned his head. "If more women would wear dresses, knee level wouldn't be such a bad place to be looking."

She shook her head very slowly. "You're a pervert, Stryker, do you know that?"

"I'm a man."

Wes thought it was very gracious of her not to say, "Same thing." Desire had been strumming through his body all day. The closer nighttime came, the tighter the knot of desire had become. He wanted her. Oh, he wouldn't have her, at least not tonight, but he wanted her to know what she was doing to him. More important, he wanted her to know how much he appreciated the way she was with the kids.

"Logan and Olivia *do* like you. Hell, the way you got

to the bottom of that missing goose mystery made you
Olivia's friend for life.''

"I'm really not—"

He rushed on as if she hadn't spoken. "But it isn't just
Olivia. Logan likes you, too. Do you know why they like
you? It's because you don't talk down to them. You're not
a fake. You don't pretend with them.''

"I don't pretend because—"

"Now I like you for a whole different set of reasons.
For one thing, I like the way you look in those hip huggers
and that waffle-weave shirt.''

The fact that his gaze had strayed to her chest probably
accounted for the quick little breath she took. It might have
even been responsible for her sudden jitters, but Wes happened to believe that there was an entirely different reason
behind the way she lowered her voice and wet her lips.

"I'm surprised at how well the clothes fit," she whispered. "Your mother must have been chesty, too.''

Wes's memories of his mother had more to do with feelings than appearance. He had a few pictures of her, so he
knew he'd gotten his hair color from her, but to be honest,
he couldn't remember very much about her chest. Jayne's
chest was a different story. He'd seen her naked breasts,
had felt them, stroked them.

"What was she like?''

Wes's heart was chugging so loud he was surprised she
couldn't hear it. He almost said, "What was who like?''
but then he realized she was asking about his mother.

He bent one knee and straightened the other, his only
concession to the change in the fit of his jeans. "Her name
was Mae, and she grew up over in Murdo, the only child
of older parents. Folks around here who knew her liked
her. My father loved her. After she died, he curled up with
a whiskey bottle most nights. I used to wonder what she
would have said if she could see us from heaven.''

"Did you ever feel her presence?" Jayne asked.

Wes shrugged. "Not really, at least not the way you hear some people tell it. Mostly, the house just felt cold and quiet and cluttered."

"Stryker," she said, placing her hand on his arm. "It's possible that you might have had a worse childhood than I did."

"Somebody's got to get the prize."

She looked at him, and he looked at her. Some prize, he thought. But as the seconds ticked by and the fire heated his back, he thought about another kind of prize, the kind a man could cozy up to at night, the kind of prize that got better over time.

After a while he said, "Are you ready to call it a day?"

She nodded, and he thought she looked beautiful with her face scrubbed free of makeup and her hair flat from the hat she'd worn outdoors and her curves tucked into clothes that hadn't been worn since the early seventies.

He hauled several more blankets to the center of the room, pulled off his boots and lowered himself to the floor a few feet from where Jayne had just done the same. He noticed that she'd turned onto her side and had closed her eyes. Several minutes passed. Wes didn't feel like sleeping. He couldn't very well do what he wanted to do, but he thought about it in vivid detail. When Olivia made a sound in her sleep, he whispered, "I'm going to give them a better childhood than either one of us had."

At first he thought she might have been asleep and hadn't heard. Until she whispered, "I'm glad, Wes."

"I believe you really are glad about that. I also believe there's a soft spot in your heart for them."

Opening her eyes, she said, "Who wouldn't like a boy and a girl who can argue the whole time they're trying to lure three half-wild barn cats out of hiding? One of these days they'll realize they don't have to fight. Right now they're probably dreaming about retaliating. I know I used to.''

"If we were alone, I'd tell you what I've been dreaming about. Better yet, I'd show you."

"You're all heart, Stryker."

He chuckled, his laughter a husky baritone, not much louder than the hiss and moan of the fire. "You're not so bad yourself. Sweet dreams, Jayne."

"You, too. 'Night, cowboy." Jayne lay awake for a long time, listening to the sigh of the wind, the occasional creak and groan of the old house, the snap of a log in the fire. She must have fallen asleep, because the world became hazy just as it always did in her dreams. Only this time, the low-lying mist that swirled all around her was accompanied by the croon of a gentle breeze that reminded her of a man's deeply drawn breath. She was on a diving board again. Rather than shining brightly, the sun flickered on the other side of her closed eyelids, and there were two children splashing in the shallow end of the pool. A man had come up behind her, his large, callused hand gliding over her from shoulder to hip, kneading, caressing, drawing a sigh from deep inside her.

She wasn't certain when she realized that it wasn't sunshine on the other side of her eyelids, but firelight, that she wasn't dreaming of the texture and the strength and the heat in the hands that were kneading her flesh. The hands were real, and the tingle along her skin wasn't a figment of her imagination.

She rolled over carefully so that she could see Wes's face in the glow of firelight. His eyes were shut, his mouth set in a straight line, his breathing deep and even. Desire fluttered and wove its way through her, stirring heat in all the usual places, and in a few unusual places, too. In her chest, for instance, and in her throat, and along the outer edges of her heart. If she and Wes had been alone, she would have slid her hand beneath his blanket and awakened him in a very erotic way. She warmed another ten degrees just thinking about it. If she and Wes had been alone she would have...

But they weren't alone. Logan and Olivia were sleeping in the same room. Even if they hadn't been in this room, they were a permanent part of Wes's life. And their well-being had to be taken into consideration. She wasn't sure what to make of the fact that they'd been in her dream.

She rolled over and curled onto her side once again, listening to the sounds of night, the low rumble of three other people's breathing, the occasional flare of the fire. Wes didn't believe children hated her. Logan and Olivia *did* seem to like her. And she had to admit she wasn't half-bad at defusing their sibling rivalry. She should know how to do that. She and Burke used to fight the same way. Maybe she wasn't bad with all kids. Maybe these two were the exception.

Maybe she could—

Maybe she could, what?

Maybe she should get some sleep and see what tomorrow brought. Releasing a breath she'd been holding—ohmygosh, Wes had been right, she did sigh—she closed her eyes and slowly drifted back to sleep.

Jayne was still thinking about her dream the next afternoon. Earlier, Wes had told her that he expected the snowplow to come through in the next day or two. He was trying to get his father's old International tractor started so he could clear a path in the driveway, and she was trying to make a dent in the snowdrift that had surrounded her car.

She leaned the snow shovel against her car, wondering about the changes that were taking place inside her. Yesterday she'd been hell-bent on getting away from this run-down ranch and the ex-rodeo champion who exasperated her and two children who terrified her. Today she wasn't exasperated or terrified or in a terrible hurry to leave.

Shading her eyes with her hand, she cast a quick glance over the snow-covered yard, where Logan and Olivia were busy building a snow fort and Wes was tinkering with the tractor near the side of the barn. She slipped into the house, added a few logs to both fires, then returned to the front stoop. She was a little surprised to find Logan sitting on the top step, waiting for her.

He'd swiped his hat off his head and was holding it in one hand. Lowering herself to a spot next to him, she said, "Did you give up on the snow fort?"

The boy shrugged. "'Livia says it's not a fort, it's a house. She always has to have her way."

Jayne refrained from mentioning that when it came to stubbornness, Logan and Olivia seemed to be of the same mold. They sat in companionable silence for a few minutes, Wes's mellow whistle carrying to their ears along with the occasional tink, tink, tink of his wrench.

"Uncle Wes sure sounds happy."

"I suppose, but talk about somebody who always has to get his own way."

Logan's silence drew Jayne's gaze. He was a handsome child with brown hair and startling dark eyebrows and lashes. He was a deep thinker who questioned and pondered nearly everything under the sun. For instance, over breakfast he'd asked who the idiot was who'd put two *r*s in February. And he saw no sense in making a bed when a person was just going to mess it up again in twelve or fourteen hours. Now, he was staring across the snow-covered yard at Wes, the serious expression on his young face making her wonder what he was considering right now.

After a while, he said, "Annabell says you can tell a lot

about a man by the sound of his whistle. Do you think that's true?''

''I suppose,'' Jayne said, but she wondered how a woman who'd gone her whole life without getting married could know so much about men. ''Annabell sounds like quite a character.''

The boy nodded. ''You'd like her. What about Uncle Wes?''

Turning her head slowly, she said, ''What about him?''

''Do you like him?''

''I suppose. Why?''

He shrugged one shoulder in that exasperating way men of all ages had. Jayne almost smiled.

''I heard Annabell talkin' on the phone to Uncle Wes a coupla weeks ago. She told him he needed a woman and me an' 'Livia needed a mother. I didn't like the sound of that, on account'a I really liked the mother I used to have and wanted her back. Plus, the only women Uncle Wes ever seemed interested in were rodeo bunnies, and I didn't even wanna think about them. But then I heard Annabell talking to the 'thorities about my aunt Meredith, and I got to thinkin' that it'd be okay if they found her and she and Uncle Wes fell in love. Then they could get married and we'd all be a family, cuz she's already related to me an' 'Livia.''

The moan of the wind and the sound of water dripping off the end of icicles and plopping to the ground faded as Jayne trained all her attention on Logan's earnest expression. She recalled Wes mentioning that Kate had a long-lost sister. Evidently the sisters were estranged, and nobody seemed to know whether Meredith was alive or dead. It would have been cruel to say that to a boy who had already lost both his parents, so Jayne said, ''Your uncle Wes loves you and Olivia, and I know for a fact that he's going to do everything he can to give you and your sister a good life. What do these rodeo bunnies look like?"

Logan let out a cackle that rivaled a seventy-year-old man's. He wiggled his eyebrows and made an hourglass shape in the air, saying, "They look like you only lots younger."

"Gee, thanks."

His eyes went round. "But they're not as smart as you. Annabell calls them buckle bunnies and says they're dumber 'n a box of rocks. I don't think Uncle Wes really likes any of them that much. He says if 'Livia ever tries to be one he'll send her to the convent."

Jayne smiled wryly, her gaze straying to the side of the barn where Wes had climbed onto the seat of the tractor and was probably begging the god of engines to let that one start. Sitting there in the waning sunlight with a boy who would undoubtedly be a heartbreaker one day, she could almost believe it was possible, not likely but possible, that she might not be so horrible with children after all. She got along pretty well with Logan and Olivia.

Hmm. Olivia.

She glanced at the yard where the girl had been playing. The snow fort or the snow house or whatever it was was empty. And so was the yard.

Jayne stood up. "Olivia," she called just as the tractor chugged to life.

"'Livia!" Logan called. "'Livia, where are you?"

The tractor sputtered and stalled. "Olivia!" Jayne called, louder than before.

Wes's head swung around, but all they heard was silence.

Jayne tried to remember how long it had been since she'd seen the child. Two minutes? Five? Ten?

What kind of trouble could a five-year-old child get into in that amount of time?

Horrible images flashed through Jayne's mind. "Olivia."

Again, there was only silence.

"Oh, my God! Olivia, where are you?"

Chapter Nine

"What's wrong?" Wes called, scanning the yard.

His attitude was no-nonsense and yet calm, and it relieved a small portion of the dread, clambering up and down Jayne's spine.

Logan yelled, "Me 'n Jayne can't find 'Livia."

Wes vaulted from the tractor and landed in the snow in one bound. "Olivia!" His voice must have traveled a mile through the still air.

The answering silence brought Jayne's dread back stronger than ever. "Olivia!" she called.

"'Livia!"

"Olivia Sue Malone, where are you?" By now, Wes had met them halfway between the house and the barn. "How long has it been since you've seen her?"

Jayne couldn't think. She tried, but she couldn't remember. Fear and dread had wrapped a fist around her windpipe, taking hold of her thought processes until she felt ten years old all over again.

What do you mean you don't know where she is? Oh,

*my God! You've lost my baby! This is all your fault. I knew
I couldn't trust you. How are your father and I supposed
to make this marriage work when I can't count on you for
anything?*

Inner torment gnawed at Jayne. Hadn't she always feared
that the past might one day repeat itself?

"Olivia!" she called with renewed vigor.

Wes made a beeline for the snow fort. He found one of
her dolls, but there was no sign of the girl. "She's got to
be here somewhere."

Of course she had to be here somewhere, Jayne thought.
Then why was she so utterly and completely terrified?

She ran all the way to the house and had checked all the
rooms downstairs by the time Logan and Wes came inside.

"She's probably hiding because I didn't want to play
stupid house with her. She's such a baby."

Wes went upstairs while Logan checked behind the
couch. "Did you find her, Uncle Wes?" the boy asked
when Wes had joined them in the living room. The shake
of his head sent a brand-new sense of dread all the way
through Jayne.

"Where did you see her last?" Wes asked.

Jayne opened her mouth to speak, but it was Logan's
voice that carried through the still air. "We were building
the snow fort, only she said it couldn't be a snow fort. It
had to be a house. I didn't want to build a sissy playhouse,
so I sat down on the stoop to wait for Jayne to come back
out."

Wes's glance in her direction prompted Jayne to say, "I
went inside to put more wood on the fire. It didn't take
more than a few minutes."

*How could you let her out of your sight? I thought you
were old enough to be trusted. Obviously I was wrong. If
anything's happened to her, I'll never forgive you. Never.*

Oh, my beautiful little girl. You've always been jealous of her. I never should have married your father.

Jayne closed her eyes against the memory, but she could still see the loathing in her stepmother's expression, could still hear the accusation in that cutting voice.

"Do you think she's hiding, Uncle Wes?"

"I don't know."

"She couldn't have been kidnapped," Logan declared. "The snowplow hasn't even been through. Besides, who'd want her? Do you think she's buried under a snowdrift?"

Jayne's hand flew to her mouth. She literally ran to the door and on outside. There were tracks everywhere, but none of them went any farther than the edge of the yard.

"We'll find her," Wes said, catching up with her by the fence he'd mended a week ago.

Jayne studied the portion of Wes's face visible beneath the brim of his gray cowboy hat. Another ten minutes had passed, and still there was no sign of Olivia. Although she couldn't be a hundred percent certain, there didn't appear to be any reproach or accusation in Wes's eyes or in the set of his mouth.

"Come on. Let's check the barn." He turned around and strode toward the weathered building a hundred yards away. Although his limp was more pronounced, she saw no evidence of anger in his stride.

He and Logan disappeared inside the barn, where they took turns calling Olivia's name. Jayne circled the entire structure before joining them. Winded, she looked in the horse stalls, even though Logan insisted he'd already checked there.

"I found her." It was Wes's voice, and it was coming from the top of the hayloft. "Come on up here, you two. You've gotta see this."

Logan went first. By the time Jayne poked her head through the opening in the floor of the hayloft, Wes and

Logan were both shaking their heads the way men had been doing for centuries. They were also both grinning at the way Olivia was lying on her side, one arm under her head, Tom the kitten tucked under the other, Marilyn and Carolyn curled up in a ball next to her. Worry drained out of Jayne so quickly it was a good thing she was holding on to the ladder with both hands.

"I wonder how she got them to sleep with her," Logan said incredulously. "Last I knew those kittens wouldn't let us anywhere near them. She's something, isn't she? 'Livia, wake up."

The girl stirred, but she didn't open her eyes.

"It looks like playing in the snow wore her out," Wes whispered. "Come on, short-stuff," he said, scooping her into his arms. "What do you say you finish this little siesta in the house? Jayne, would you get Snuggles? Jayne?"

She felt Wes's eyes on her. Although it required a conscious effort to pull herself together, she grabbed the stuffed toy and followed him to the ladder.

At the bottom he said, "Are you okay?"

Okay? Of course she was okay. "I'm fine," she said, looking past Wes's shoulder. "I just had a flashback, that's all."

Her voice must have sounded more brittle than she'd intended, because even the dog had turned to look at her strangely. Pulling herself together, she brushed past Wes, waiting to close the door until everyone else had gone through.

She was thankful that the others didn't appear to notice how slow her steps were as she trailed them to the house. By the time she let herself in the back door, Wes had already laid Olivia on the couch. "Logan," he said quietly, handing the boy a pail. "Fill this with clean snow, would you?"

Logan accepted the bucket along with the chore and went

outside. Now that they were alone, Wes turned to Jayne. "What's wrong?"

Since there was really no reason *not* to look at him, Jayne forced herself to turn around and meet his gaze. "Nothing's wrong. I'm fine, really. Why do you ask?"

"Because you look like you've just seen a ghost, for one thing. And what did you mean out there when you said you'd just had a flashback?"

"Did I say that?"

There it was again. That brittle edge in Jayne's voice. Wes felt on the verge of understanding something very important about her. "Yes," he said. "You did say that. What did you mean?"

"It was nothing, really."

"I'll be the judge of that."

"I really don't—"

"I do." He shot her a penetrating look and assumed his most stubborn stance, his legs spread a comfortable distance apart, feet planted, shoulders back, arms crossed. "How old were you in this flashback?"

"You're a bully, Stryker, do you know that?"

"So you've said. How old?"

"I was ten, and it isn't a big deal."

He lowered his chin and his voice. "And what happened when you were ten years old?"

She shrugged one shoulder, then walked past him, pausing in the doorway where she stared at Olivia who was still sleeping.

"We were on vacation, Burke and I, our dad and his second, no, his third wife, and her four-year-old daughter. Dad and Suzanne had been fighting for months. The trip to the zoo was supposed to make everything better, only my stepsister wandered away when I was supposed to be watching her. It was awful. Everybody was screaming and crying.

The police came, the exits were sealed, and the whole zoo was searched. Emily wasn't there.''

"Where was she?"

"A childless couple from Florida had found her. The FBI picked them up in Utah. At their trial, they said they believed finding Emily had been a gift from God. Luckily they hadn't harmed her, but Suzanne never spoke to me again.''

"And she and your father?"

"They divorced soon after the incident.''

Wes shook his head. "Good for him.''

She shrugged. "Stepmother number four wasn't much better. My father really has terrible taste in women. Anyway, now you know the details of my sordid past.''

He placed his hands on her shoulders and gently drew her against him so that her shoulder blades touched his chest. "Relax,'' he whispered against her hair. "I'll bet even Wicked Witch Number Three knew it wasn't your fault. You were too young to be responsible for a four-year-old. Hell, you were too young to be responsible for yourself.''

He sensed that she wanted to let her guard down and lean against him but something held her back. Gliding his hands around her waist, he spread his fingers wide, slowly inching his way to her ribs, until his fingers closed partway over her soft, perfectly shaped breasts. His breathing grew so ragged it took a moment for a sound in the distance to register.

Jayne turned her head. "Is that a train?'' she whispered.

There was a knock on the window behind them, and Logan's excited squeal as he said, "Jayne, Uncle Wes, look. The snowplow's coming!''

Jayne was out of his arms in a flash, slipping past him so quickly she stirred up a cold breeze.

"What are you doing?'' he called.

"I'm getting out of here."

She was fast. So fast, in fact, that he barely had time to stick his foot in the bathroom door when she tried to close it tight.

"Move your stupid foot, Stryker."

"No."

She yanked the door open. Glaring at him, she said, "What? You want to watch?"

Before he could answer, she shook the wrinkles out of the black skirt she'd been wearing when she'd arrived and hurriedly pulled it on over his mother's old jeans. She toed out of the boots he'd loaned her and promptly removed the jeans.

He raised his eyebrows slightly when she reached for the hem of the faded knit shirt, curiosity and a healthy dose of masculine interest filtering past his anger. Leaning a hip against the door frame, he settled in to enjoy the show.

Her lips thinned, her eyes flashing with insolence. She turned around at the last minute, so that he had to imagine the way her soft, plump breasts he'd just held in his hands looked covered in beige lace.

"It's probably for the best that this happened now," she said, pulling that ridiculous sweater with the fake fur trim over her head. "Any later, and I might have actually fallen in love with you." She took what appeared to be a lace-topped, thigh-high nylon stocking, black, of course, in her hands. When she glided that stocking up her leg, Wes forgot to breathe. He didn't fare any better watching her pull on the other one.

"Although how I could even consider falling in love with a man who doesn't begin to know the meaning of the word *gentleman* is beyond me." She was leaning down now, buckling the strap of a clunky-healed shoe. "As it is, all that's between us is attraction. An instinctive drive that causes people to do instinctive, mindless things."

"That's not all that's between us, dammit."

"Of course it is."

"No, it's not Jayne."

"Yes, it is."

"It isn't."

She pushed her hair behind her ears and rolled her eyes. "Listen to us. We're as bad as Logan and Olivia."

"Jayne."

She spun around, stopping directly in front of him. Her gaze held his, and she wet her lips. Wes held his breath, his blood heating. As she raised up on tiptoe his vision blurred and his eyes closed. He felt another flutter of cold air, and, damn, she slipped past him before he had the sense to open his eyes.

"Where the hell are you going? Get back and fight like a—"

She turned at the door. Coat in hand, she said, "Like a what? See? You don't even know what you're saying."

He followed as far as the back stoop, then stood watching as she traipsed through the snow in a skirt and silk stockings—he swallowed with difficulty—and shoes. Grabbing the snow shovel she'd leaned against her car earlier, she attacked the drift covering half of the front of her car.

"You want to leave?" he shouted. *Darn fool woman, anyway.* "Fine. Go."

"I will."

"Good. I don't like prickly women, anyway, and you're as prickly as they come."

"Tell me something I don't already know." She scooped up another shovelful of snow.

"I don't like short hair, either," he said, swearing at the pain shooting through his knee when he stomped closer. "Plus, you dress weird, and another thing—"

She glanced up at him as if she was about to say something equally scathing, but she bit her lip and shook her head, gesturing to the stoop where Logan and Olivia were both standing.

"They're scared, Wes. They've been through so much."

"They're tough, resilient." Tougher and more resilient than she'd been at that age. He lowered his voice. "Jayne, you really were too young to be held responsible for what happened to your stepsister."

"Maybe. But I should have been old enough today. Those kids need a mother," she said shakily. "And I've just realized that I'd like to help."

The anger that had been coiled inside Wes uncurled like a lasso sailing out over its target. He took another step toward her, thinking this was more like it. She might have been prickly, but she had a gentle side, too. And her hair might have been short, but not too short. And her eyes, well...

"You need a wife, Stryker."

Right now he would have liked a quiet room and a little privacy. And her.

"I could help you find one if you'd like."

The snowplow's engine faded away in the distance, until the only sounds Wes heard were the wind and his own blood rushing through his head. "What did you say?" he asked.

She wet her lips, stuck the shovel in the drift and calmly met his gaze. "I said I'll help you find a wife."

Now wait just a cotton-picking minute....

"It won't be any trouble. I used to be in advertising, and I know nearly every angle and approach. It shouldn't be that difficult, really. You aren't bad looking, and you do have a certain amount of cowboy brawn that probably appeals to a lot of women. You're tall, and you're hardworking, but not too hardworking. You seem to know how to have a good time, too. You know what they say about all work and no play. And you have a sense of humor. Some women find that very attractive in a man.''

Some women? Wes felt his eyes narrow. Why was Jayne talking so fast? She was rambling. And she never rambled. Was she nervous? Or afraid? What was she afraid of?

Love?

Was that it? Yes, that was it, or at least that was close. She liked him. Oh, she didn't want to. She especially didn't want to fall in love with him.

She was still talking. Wes decided to use the time it took her to finish to formulate a plan.

"And your hair hasn't started to thin, yet. Plus, you're tall. Many a woman's head has been turned by a tall…''

"Jayne?"

"…man. What?''

"You already said that."

Her blue eyes darkened noticeably. And she swallowed. "I did?"

He nodded.

"Oh. In that case, I guess I've said everything there is to say."

Not quite, Wes thought.

"Wes?"

"Hmm?"

"Did you fix the tractor?"

"The tractor?''

She nodded. "Yes. The tractor. Does it run? Because if it does, I would appreciate it if you would use it to pull my car out of this drift. Otherwise I'll be here all night and half of tomorrow."

Wes ran a hand over his eyes, down his cheeks, across his chin. Nothing about the conversation should have been lust arousing, and yet his desire for Jayne had never been stronger. The closer he came to knowing her, the more certain he was that she was the woman for him. Her. Not one of the other single women in Jasper Gulch. Tipping up the brim of his Stetson, he said, ''I could probably keep the tractor running long enough to pull your car out to the road, but first, tell me how you're planning to go about finding a woman for me.''

''Not just a woman,'' she said, warming to the subject. ''I offered to help you find a wife. That advertisement the area ranchers put in the papers a few years ago is still hanging in the diner. When the newspapers ran the story, there were only six marriageable women and sixty-two bachelors in Jasper Gulch, right? I believe that some of the women who came to town married a few of those bachelors, and a few of the local girls have tied the knot, too. Has anybody done the math recently? Never mind. I'll get the information I need from Louetta and Melody. I'll have to ask you a few questions concerning the type of woman you're looking for. After that, it'll just be a matter of setting up interviews and relaying the information to you. Of course, it'll be up to you to take it from there.''

''Then what you're saying is that if I agree to do this, you'll agree to work closely with me.''

It was her turn to narrow her eyes suspiciously. ''I suppose.''

Wes almost grinned.

''Where are you going?'' she asked.

He glanced over his shoulder. ''You said you wanted me to get the tractor running, didn't you?''

She nodded, but she still looked suspicious.

He was walking backward, which wasn't easy in the deep snow. ''The tractor won't start without me. When were you planning to begin interviewing these potential wives?''

''I'll begin working on it as soon as I get back to town. I have to put together the plan I proposed to the town council and the Ladies Aid Society, too, but I should be able to work on both projects simultaneously.''

Wes didn't appreciate being called a *project,* but if it meant she would continue to see him, what the hell. ''Then you'll keep me posted?''

''Keep you posted?'' Jayne glanced up sharply, her whole demeanor growing in severity. Until she'd come to Jasper Gulch, she'd never repeated things people said.

''Good,'' he said, as if she'd agreed to his suggestion. He turned around and jauntily made his way to the side of the barn where the tractor had quit years ago. She wasn't certain what she'd just let herself in for, but when his mellow whistle carried to her ears, she knew he had something up his sleeve.

She shook off the notion, reminding herself that what she was doing, she was doing for the good of everyone. Her, Wes, the kids. Especially the kids. She wasn't a fanciful woman. She knew that. She also knew her strengths and her weaknesses. The brush she'd had with Olivia's disappearance had reminded her of the latter. She was a modern-day woman with a smart mouth, a nose for success and an honest soul.

She honestly didn't know what to do about that blasted whistle.

She spun around and came face-to-face with Logan and Olivia, who were watching with uncharacteristic quietude from the stoop. They desperately needed a mother. Jayne knew what she had to do. Really, she'd known it all along. She was going to have to ignore the yearnings Wes stirred up inside her. More important, she was going to have to find a woman who would appreciate a man like him, a man who could whistle and argue and who didn't bat at eye at the prospect of raising two children who sometimes appeared to be precocious and as wily as sailors but were really angels in disguise.

"Hi," Jayne said, stepping up to the first step a few feet from the kids.

"What's Uncle Wes doing?" Olivia asked.

Logan made a disparaging sound of disgust. "If you had half a brain you could see that he's startin' the tractor. Are you blind or what?"

"I'm not blind, and I do so have half a brain."

"You just admitted that you only have half a brain."

"Did not."

"Did so."

"Did not."

"Tell her, Jayne."

Jayne eyed the two—gulp—angels in disguise, and slowly released her breath through pursed lips. Heaven help her. She had her work cut out for her.

"Here, try this."

"No, thanks, Wes. I'm full. Really. Oh, all right. Mmm."

"Not bad, huh?" Wes asked, popping a morsel of breaded chicken into his own mouth. "Especially if you consider how long it's probably been frozen. Thank goodness for microwaves."

Jayne swallowed and shook her head. "I try not to think about where a microwave dinner has been or about the whole microwave process. What do you think about Tracy Gentry?"

Wes propped his elbows on the table and tried to hide his annoyance. Jayne had stopped by an hour ago with her list of prospective brides. It had taken some fancy talking on his part to convince her to stay while he finished up in the barn. She'd followed him into the house fifteen minutes ago and had launched into her spiel the second she'd taken off her coat. Standing behind her, Wes had peered over her shoulder as she'd given a brief rundown on every woman in town between the ages of twenty-one and fifty. It wasn't his fault he couldn't concentrate. He hadn't had a coherent thought since he'd gotten his first whiff of her perfume.

Since his microwave dinner had already been cooking, he'd insisted she stay for lunch, even though it was the middle of the afternoon. They'd eaten together while she'd shown him her graphs and charts and her notebook containing the data she'd collected. She'd even run background checks and had highlighted areas of mutual interest. She was thorough, he had to give her that.

He wanted to give her a kiss. Right on those lips she'd tinted a deep plum to match the angora sweater she was wearing with a pair of enticing, tight black jeans.

It had been a week since the snowplow had come through, and although he'd spoken with her often on the phone, this was the first time he'd seen her in person since she'd agreed to help him find a wife.

"Wes?"

"What?"

"I asked you what you thought about Tracy Gentry?"

He took a sip of coffee that had sat in the pot too long and said, "Isn't she a little young?"

"She's over twenty-one."

"By what, a month?"

Jayne shrugged. "Beggars can't be choosers. Tracy's pretty, and you seem to have a preference for well-endowed women."

Pretending his scowl was meant for the bitter coffee, he pushed the cup out of his way. He didn't have a preference for just *any* well-endowed woman, dammit. He had a preference for the well-endowed woman sitting across from him right now.

"Well?" she prodded.

He took his time meeting her gaze. "Did I mention that the social worker made her home visit this morning?"

Jayne felt a headache coming on. These sudden changes in topics were making her dizzy. Still, her curiosity got the best of her, and she had to ask, "How did it go?"

He looked at her in a manner that let her know he didn't think there should have been any doubt how it had gone. Jayne rolled her eyes, but she found herself smiling. "Really, Wes. It would make things a lot easier if you would answer my questions the first time I ask."

"She said I passed inspection with flying colors."

"Was this social worker single?"

This time he only shrugged one shoulder. "I didn't ask."

"Why not?"

"She outweighed me, for one thing. And she had a five-o'clock shadow."

"Surely you're exaggerating."

"It was ten-thirty in the morning."

Jayne smiled. "I can see where that might be a problem."

"I figured you'd see it my way."

She riffled through her notes. "Let's see. If you're looking for a slightly more mature woman, preferably one who doesn't shave, you should give Josie Callahan or Crystal Galloway a call. They're both relatively new to Jasper Gulch. And they're both over twenty-one. I had a little trouble getting close to Crystal Galloway, but Josie Callahan is open and warm. She has a little girl, so I know she loves children. According to the Jasper Gulch grapevine, she..."

While Jayne continued to sing Josie Callahan's praises, Wes settled himself more comfortably in his chair. He tried to listen, but his mind wandered, his thoughts turning hazy, conjuring up images that were arousing and sensual and—

"Stryker, are you even listening?"

He came out of his fantasies to find Jayne's eyes flashing

knowingly. "Did I tell you that Logan and Olivia both like school?"

"Wes, I'm trying to make a little headway with these prospective brides."

He leaned ahead. "Olivia likes school because she likes her teacher. Logan has a different reason."

"What reason?"

"He has a crush."

"On a girl?"

"No, on the school's hamster. Of course on a girl."

"Did he tell you that?"

"Not in so many words. But he hasn't stopped talking about Haley Carson since the first day of school. And last night he asked how a boy knows when to kiss a girl."

"What did you tell him?"

"What could I tell him? I'm still waiting for somebody to give me a few pointers. You wouldn't happen to know anyone who might volunteer for the job, would you?"

He eased closer. Not close enough to kiss her, but close enough to make her the tiniest bit uncomfortable and a whole lot aware. "Josie Callahan or Crystal Galloway might."

"Does anybody else come to mind?" he asked.

Outside, brakes hissed and squeaked. From the corner of her eye, she saw the school bus drive away, Tyrone nipping at the kids' heels all the while they ran toward the house. Within seconds the door banged open and Logan and Olivia burst into the house.

Wes drew away slightly at the intrusion. Jayne would have felt better if he had taken the awareness arcing between them with him.

"Is that chicken I smell?" Logan asked, sniffing the air.

Wes hung the coats the kids had shrugged out of on pegs near the door. Olivia was in a chatty mood, but Logan was more interested in the chicken nuggets Wes had reheated and placed in front of him. There was something appealing about the whole thing. Jayne didn't want to enjoy it, but she couldn't help it. Maybe sitting across a kitchen table from a blue-eyed cowboy while two kids ate chicken with their fingers was enough to make anybody feel relaxed and content.

She drew back slightly at the way Logan smacked his food and licked his fingers. One happenstance glance at Wes changed the beating rhythm of her heart all over again. Soft-touched thoughts shaped her smile. After several long seconds, he smiled in return.

A warning sounded in her brain. She managed to pull her gaze away and immediately began gathering up her notes and charts. She'd done her homework before coming out here today. She'd waited a week, giving herself plenty of time to get her bearings before paying Wes a little visit. She'd even listened to the weather report. This time she'd vowed not to take any chances.

If she didn't get out of there very soon, there was a chance she wouldn't want to leave. Bristling, she tucked her papers into the briefcase she'd brought with her and carefully rose to her feet. "You really should consider paying a little visit to Josie's flower shop. Buy a bouquet of flowers."

With her hand on the doorknob, she cast one last glance over her shoulder at the three people who were sitting at the table. The kids' attention was trained on their snack, but Wes's eyes were on her. "Why flowers?" he asked.

"Because sometimes," she said quietly, "a bouquet of flowers is the nicest thing that can happen to a woman."

Without another word, she left.

Wes strode to the window. Standing back far enough so she couldn't see him, he watched until her car drove out of sight. Normally, she had the go-to-hell haughtiness of one of his barn cats. She'd been different today. She obviously liked flowers. That was nice. Flowers were nice. But no matter what she'd said, they shouldn't be the nicest thing that happened to a woman. *He* wanted to be the nicest thing that happened to her, dammit.

It was amazing how a woman who was so bossy and stubborn could also be so blind. He paused, his thoughts taking an interesting turn, his imaginary caveman club taking on an entirely different form.

She thought he should pay a little visit to the flower shop. He'd never been very good at taking orders. Suddenly he could hardly wait to do exactly as Jayne said.

Well, maybe not exactly.

Chapter Ten

It was almost five o'clock, and Jayne was staring at the pages spread out on the dining room table. Using her hands to block out everything in her peripheral vision, she tried again to read her own writing. The words swam before her eyes.

Normally she didn't have this much trouble concentrating. The plan she was proposing to the town council concerning the need for new businesses and career opportunities for the women in the area should have been challenging enough to hold her interest.

She took a calming breath, and her eyes, the traitors, fluttered closed at the heady, heavenly scent of flowers wafting on the air. She clamped her mouth shut, pushed away from the table and paced as far away from the flowers as she could get.

What had Wes been thinking? When she'd suggested that he buy flowers four days ago, she'd meant for *Josie,* not for her. Who in their right mind would put lavender and larkspur with a bouquet of red roses, anyway? The air in her small house had been full of the strangely alluring scent ever since those flowers had been delivered early that very morning by Josie Callahan, herself.

Jayne had opened her door, smiling at the shy, red-haired woman standing on her front porch. When Josie had handed over the bouquet, Jayne had been speechless. And she was *never* speechless. She'd managed to pull herself together enough to stammer out a thank-you of sorts, but she'd been trying to figure out what Josie's pert little wink had meant ever since.

What was Wes trying to do? She couldn't begin to fathom what went on in the convoluted recesses of his mind. No wonder he was still single. She had half a notion to tell him that. Since she was a woman who learned from her mistakes, she knew better than to drive out to the ranch to give that ex-rodeo champion a piece of her mind.

It was too bad, too. She would have enjoyed that.

Heaving a huge sigh, she decided to give the proposal she was working on another try. She was halfway to the kitchen when the telephone rang. She reached for the cordless phone on her way by, her steps coming to a complete stop the instant that slight Western drawl reached her ear.

"What did you think of the flowers?"

Wes. Jayne could have done without the slow dip her heart took into her stomach, but she had to hand it to herself for her speedy recovery. "Are you nuts? You were supposed to ask Josie out. Now she's going to be convinced there's something going on between you and me. Which is ridiculous. Sending me flowers really wasn't a very bright thing to do."

"For your information I sent them to you out of appreciation for all the work you did on behalf of my prospective wives."

"Oh. I told you it was no trouble. Still, I'm afraid you're sending out the wrong message to the single women in town. How do you think Josie felt delivering flowers to me when you were supposed to ask her out for a night on the—''

"Josie and I went out."

"You did?" she asked, and then, before she could stop herself, "When?"

"Two nights ago."

"Then you should have sent *her* flowers, not me. Would you want to go on a second date with a man who sent another woman flowers the day after *your* first date with him?"

"To tell you the truth, I can't imagine going on a first date with a man."

Jayne shook her head. "I was merely being philosophical. You should try it sometime."

Wes ran a hand across his eyes, thinking that a lesser man would crumble beneath that woman's sharp tongue. Luckily for him, he wasn't a lesser man. "Jayne, I didn't call to be abused, although I admit that I've always wondered how it would feel to be pummeled with a woman's high-heeled shoe."

"Can it, Stryker. Why did you call, anyway?"

"I need a favor."

"What kind of favor?"

Wes stretched his legs out in front of him and smiled at the suspicion in her voice. He wasn't fond of being insulted, but he rather enjoyed being the object of Jayne's suspicions.

"I have a date tonight and my baby-sitter just canceled."

"Really?"

"She has the flu or something."

"I didn't mean that. I meant, do you really have a date tonight?"

"You don't have to sound so surprised. Dating was the

whole purpose behind all that data you collected on the single women in town, wasn't it?"

"Yes, of course. Are you seeing Josie again?"

"No. Josie Callahan is very sweet, and so is her daughter. That's the problem."

"You don't like sweet women?"

"No. I mean, yes, I like them just fine." He groaned deep in his throat. "It's just that Josie's afraid Logan and Olivia will eat her little girl alive."

"Oh."

"Exactly. So I called Crystal Galloway."

"You did? I mean, good."

On his end of the telephone, Wes smiled again. "At least you think I'm capable of doing something right."

"Wes, I didn't mean to—"

"About that favor."

She was silent for a moment. Dang, but it was amazing how much fun it was to try to stay one step ahead of her.

"What do you need, Wes?"

"Would you mind watching the kids for a few hours?"

"Tonight?"

"Unless you have other plans."

Jayne glanced at the notes spread out on the table and at the frozen dinner she'd planned to microwave later. "I'm not doing anything that can't be postponed, Wes, but—"

"Good. Can you be here around six?"

"Really, Wes, I'm not a good candidate to keep an eye on those two kids."

"I'll put all the knives and flammable material on a high shelf."

"Very funny."

"Olivia wants to show you the trick she taught Tyrone, and Logan wants to show you his shiner."

"His what?" she gasped.

"You heard right. It seems he tried to kiss Haley Carson, and she hauled off and smacked him a good one."

Jayne shook her head. "It sounds like true love."

"That's what I told him. I'll see you at six. Oh, Jayne?"

She raised the phone back to her ear in time to hear Wes say, "You never said what you thought of the flowers."

Staring at the bouquet of flowers, Jayne's mouth went dry and her heart skipped a beat. When she felt she'd regained enough of her equilibrium to speak, she said, "I think that if somebody could find a way to bottle that scent, they would make a fortune."

His chuckle carried to only one ear, yet the warmth it evoked made her weak in the knees. The line went dead while she was still holding the phone.

She punched the off button by rote. *That man was getting to her.* Nonsense, she sputtered to herself while she put the frozen dinner back in the freezer then changed into a pair of brown jeans and a chartreuse sweater. He in no way, shape or form was getting to her. She was still sputtering when she donned her brightest and reddest coat and started to open the door. A thread of caution had her turning around and reaching for the remote control, which she aimed at the television and promptly punched up the weather channel.

Partly sunny, cold and windy—surprise, surprise—but not a flake of snow was predicted. She commended herself for her good sense, then turned off the television. She had to walk past that bouquet on her way to the door. Her feet came to a stop. Leaning over, she slowly touched the tip of her nose to the delicate petals of larkspur, lavender and roses.

Wes pulled his shiny silver truck into the barn and hopped out. He didn't pay a lot of attention to the fancy bucking bronco painted on the door. Most of his attention

was turned inward as he rehearsed what he would say to
the woman who was waiting for him in the house.

He'd been looking forward to this moment for the past
two hours, ever since he'd dropped Crystal off early and
had headed over to the Crazy Horse to kill some time.

The kitchen light was on. He'd noticed that before he'd
turned into the driveway. Quietly letting himself in the back
door, he found the rest of the house nearly dark. He
shrugged out of his coat and hat and hung them on the peg
automatically. Avoiding the more serious creaks in the
kitchen floor, he strode to the doorway of the living room.
He paused for a moment, his eyes adjusting to the dim
interior. The television was on in the corner, its silver glow
the only source of illumination in the entire room. It was
all the light he needed to pick out the shapes sprawled out
on either end of the sofa, and the woman who had nodded
off in the easy chair in the corner.

He nearly tripped over the dog, who let out a little yelp
at the rude awakening. Regaining his balance, Wes made
his way toward that easy chair, half wondering if a half-
wild kitten or two might streak past any minute.

He went down on his haunches about the same time
Jayne opened her eyes. "How was your date?" she asked.

He shrugged. "Okay, I guess. What's Tyrone doing in
the house."

Her head jerked toward the kids. "They assured me you
said it would be all right."

Score one for the kids. Wes's gaze swept over Jayne's
face, stilling on her eyes for a moment, then dipping to her
lips. A muscle moved in her throat. An answering one
moved in his. Now, if only he could score one with Jayne.

"Did you and Crystal have a nice time?" she whispered.

Wes tried to decide how to answer. Crystal Galloway
was a knockout. She had wavy blond hair and exotic green
eyes. She was bright, articulate and exuded feminine sen-

suality. They'd both known fifteen minutes into the date that there wasn't going to be a second.

"Wes?" Jayne prodded.

He met her gaze and shrugged again. "I don't think she likes me. Can you believe that?"

She inclined her head slightly, her voice laced with warmth and humor. "My, that is a stretch of the imagination."

"That's what I thought."

She rose to her feet in one fluid motion, blithely striding into the kitchen. Wes rose twice as slowly and a lot more stiffly. By the time he joined her in the next room, she'd pushed her hair out of her eyes and seemed to be trying to wake up completely.

"How did things go around here?" he asked, stopping a few feet away from her.

"Pretty well, actually. You missed the show. Clayt and Melody Carson brought Haley over and made her apologize for giving Logan a black eye. I think you were right. I think it is true love. Speaking of true love, I think you should give Tracy Gentry a call."

He shook his head in a manner that left no doubt that he was serious.

"You've already had dinner with Josie and Crystal and you said you had lunch with Jackie Parker. Unless you want to give Addie and Gussie Cunningham, both of whom exceed the age limit of fifty that you specified at the beginning, I'm afraid you're list of prospective brides is depleted."

"Jayne?"

She blamed the sleep that was surely still in her eyes for the way her vision turned hazy. She tried blinking, but once Wes's lips touched hers, she couldn't seem to pry her eyes open. Her lips, on the other hand, opened automatically.

The kiss was soft at first, turning greedy and hot and

explosive. Her hands went to his shoulders, his wound around her back, one high, the other low, drawing her closer, closer, his lips moving over hers all the while. She should have gasped at the evidence of his desire. She reveled in it instead, moving against him, sighing, kissing him in return.

He ended the kiss gradually, degree by degree, inch by inch, until only his forehead touched hers. She opened her eyes, swallowed and finally rasped, ''Why did you do that?''

''I've been wanting to for days.''

She stepped out of his arms and instantly felt cold. ''But your dates with Crystal and Josie—''

''Didn't work out.''

''But there aren't any other single women in the entire county who—''

''There's you.''

''Oh, no you don't,'' she sputtered. ''I told you up front that I wasn't looking for a relationship. I'm finished with men, remember?''

He was holding her coat like some gentleman, when she knew darn well no gentleman would try to get away with kissing a woman senseless one minute and the next whispering, ''Who are you trying to convince, Jayne? Me? Or you?''

''Think of Logan and Olivia,'' she said, opening the door. ''I know what it's like to have stepmothers who had no business becoming mothers in the first place.''

She was still talking when she reached her car. ''Those two kids in there need the kind of woman born to be a mother, and you and I both know—''

''What those kids need is love,'' he said, holding the door while she slid onto the seat.

''Of course they need love.''

''Face it, Jayne. You love those two hellions and you'd

like nothing better than to mother them. But kids aren't the only ones who need love.''

With that massive bit of understatement, he closed her door and calmly strode into the house.

Jayne must have started her car. When she arrived back at her place, she had no recollection of the fifteen-mile drive. Her mind was blank. She was stunned.

The first thing she noticed when she let herself into her house was the scent of roses and lavender. She squared her jaw, and since she couldn't glare at Wes, she transferred her aggression to the innocent blooms. Shrugging out of her coat, she paced. And she thought. And she called Wesley Engelbert Stryker every name in the book. It was possible that she might have created a few new ones, as well.

She went to bed, eventually, and was relieved at how comfortable her bed felt, how warm and soft the blankets were, and quickly her thoughts turned hazy and her body became weightless. She was going to dream again. In that moment before sleep came, she tried to picture the swimming pool, tried to imagine the feel of the sun, so hot on her back.

She dreamed. Only this dream was different. It was hazier, more difficult to follow. Instead of standing on a diving board, she found herself peering at a big, heavy door. The sign said Doctor's Office. She walked inside a room that looked suspiciously like the Crazy Horse Saloon. It was dimly lit and smelled faintly of roses and lavender. Someone called her name, and she turned to find a doctor who was a dead ringer for DoraLee Brown.

"Hop up on the bar. I mean examining table," the bleached blond doctor said.

After a few tut-tuts and hmms, the DoraLee look-alike said, "Good news, sugar. It's twins."

There was a sound, like a zipper unzipping. The next thing Jayne knew, Logan and Olivia popped out of her stomach and immediately started arguing over who was first.

Head pounding, thoughts screaming, Jayne bolted to a sitting position. Oh, my gosh. Wes was right. She *did* want to be those kids' mother. She broke out in a cold sweat.

She paced the rest of the night. By daybreak she knew what she had to do.

The nerves that were tap dancing up and down Jayne's spine quieted somewhat the moment she spotted Logan and Olivia sitting on the fence Wes had mended a few weeks earlier. It was sunny, and the meteorologist she'd listened to during the drive out here was predicting a January thaw. Jayne's hands were clammy, and it had nothing to do with the sudden appearance of the sun.

Olivia waved so hard she teetered on the top of the fence. Jayne's heart wedged itself in her throat at the sight of the little girl toppling to the ground. Olivia hopped to her feet, the expression on her face making it clear that the only thing injured was her pride. Wes had been right. These kids were tough and resilient. He was right about how she felt about them, too. She had to tell him, before she lost her nerve. If he said, "I told you so," she might be forced to kiss him right there in the yard in front of Logan and Olivia and the animals and God and everyone.

As if thoughts of Wes conjured him up, he stepped out of the barn and into the sunshine. The sight of the tall, willowy blonde holding his hand stopped Jayne cold.

At first she thought it was Crystal Galloway, but upon closer inspection, Jayne saw that this woman's hair was longer and perfectly straight and the color of spun gold.

Logan opened Jayne's door, both kids talking up a blue streak at the same time. Interspersed with gibberish she couldn't understand were two words. "Aunt Meredith."

Grinning for all they were worth, Logan and Olivia each

took one of Jayne's hands and pulled her around to the front of her car where she came face-to-face with Wes. And the kids' Aunt Meredith. Meredith, who had been their mother's long-lost sister. Meredith, who was related by blood to Logan and Olivia. Meredith, who Logan had admitted he'd wanted to marry Wes.

The dog nudged Jayne's knee with his head, drawing her gaze. He looked up at her soulfully and wagged his tail. Thankful for the moment's reprieve from her own screaming thoughts and questions, Jayne reached into her oversize pocket and unwrapped a steak bone. "It's okay to like the treats," she said, scratching his head. "But you're starting to expect them, and that's not very polite."

She straightened. Having run out of diversions, she met Wes's gaze. Pasting a smile on her face, she said, "I brought more treats out for the animals." And then, even though she almost choked on her tongue, she forced herself to be polite, almost nice even, to the woman who was watching her openly.

"Hello. The kids tell me you're their aunt Meredith. I'm Jayne Kincaid. I've been trying to help this stubborn cowboy here find a suitable wife."

"Kate used to do that, too," Meredith said, her voice deep and sultry and, darn it all, sad.

Jayne's heart ached a little around the edges. She might have been able to retaliate, or at the very least regroup, if the other woman hadn't been so hauntingly beautiful, if her eyes, so like Logan's and Olivia's, hadn't been so dark and sad. Jayne would bow out gracefully. Yes, that's what she would do.

Shading her eyes with one hand, she said, "Such a nice day."

"Yes," Meredith agreed. "Beautiful. Wes says it's going to get muddy, though."

"Yes, I suppose so," Jayne agreed amicably. "Isn't he

doing a nice job on the ranch?'' And she responded automatically to Meredith's comment. ''Oh, you like this skirt? How nice of you to say so.... Yes, Jasper Gulch is a nice, quiet town.''

She excused herself to feed the other animals. She could feel Wes's eyes on her, but she didn't allow herself to meet his gaze again. Watching very carefully for her chance to escape, she waited until Wes, Meredith and the kids were near the house. Speed-walking to her car, she called, ''Goodbye, everyone.''

''Jayne, wait!'' Wes protested.

''I can't,'' Jayne said. ''It was nice meeting you, Meredith.'' Without a backward glance she drove away.

Chapter Eleven

Wes had to wait until late afternoon to drive into town. Of all days, he'd had an appointment to keep with the social worker, and Meredith had wanted to know all the details regarding Kate and Dusty's accident, about their last words and where they'd been laid to rest. To top it all off, Dusty's favorite horse had chosen today to break through a weak section of fence. It had taken Wes two hours to track him down and bring him home.

He'd thought about Jayne's behavior the entire time. He didn't get it. The woman who'd visited the ranch that very morning had looked like Jayne. She'd had dark hair that had skimmed her eyebrows and brushed the edges of her jaw; wide, blue eyes and a generous mouth. She'd even sounded like Jayne.

But who in the hell had that meek-and-mild lady been?

He pulled his muddy silver truck to a stop in front of the little house on Elm Street and jumped out. He stormed up to the porch and entered without bothering to knock. "All right," he bellowed after he'd stomped up every stair and found Jayne in one of the bedrooms on the second floor. "Who are you and what have you done with the woman I love?"

Jayne stared at him. He was already in love with Meredith?

She'd heard the squeal of tires rounding the corner and had peeked out the window as Wes had slammed on the brakes in front of her house. She'd had a good minute and a half to prepare herself for seeing him again. It really ticked her off that she felt so much like crying. Carefully folding the sweater that was in her hand, she placed it in a suitcase before turning her head and looking at Wes.

"She was with you when I left this morning. It isn't my problem if you can't keep track of your women. Please excuse me. As you can see, I have more packing to do."

For a moment Wes felt the way he used to when he'd landed on the ground so hard it rattled his teeth and stunted his thoughts. But then he recovered, and he realized that she thought he'd been talking about *Meredith* when he'd referred to the woman he loved.

He felt a grin coming on. Dang, he felt a lot more than that. Jayne had been trying to be *nice*. Imagine that.

Lifting the brim of his hat a quarter of an inch or so, he ambled a little closer. "I'm not talking about Meredith, you idiot. She only learned of Kate's and Dusty's deaths a few days ago. She and Kate hadn't spoken in years, but she wanted to see for herself that the kids are okay. She's thinking about staying on in Jasper Gulch, but she doesn't want to disrupt Logan's and Olivia's lives. She doesn't want to disrupt my life, either. And if you say that's nice, I'm going to throttle you. You're nuts, do you know that? But I happen to be in love with you."

Jayne had straightened sometime during Wes's little tirade. Redistributing her weight to one foot, she folded her arms and cocked her head. "Why don't you come over here and say that?"

Wes stared at her from the middle of the room, heart pounding, mind reeling. The next thing he knew, he had her in his arms, and his hands all over her. He kissed her lips, her cheek, her jaw. Through it all, she managed to say, "I wasn't packing to leave Jasper Gulch, Stryker."

"You weren't?" he asked, his mouth covering hers all over again.

She waited to answer until after the long, searing kiss had ended. As was so typical of her, she picked up right where she'd left off. "After all, *I'm* not the idiot, here. I planned to show up on your doorstep with my suitcases in hand. And I wasn't going to check the weather channel, either. Maybe Meredith is related to those kids, but she couldn't love them any more than I do. And even if there was a history between the two of you, she couldn't love you any more than I do, either."

"You love me?" he asked, his voice a mere whisper.

She rolled her eyes. "God only knows why, but of course I love you."

"And you were going to drive out to the ranch and fight for me?"

A grin slid across her lips. An answering smile stole over his. "Shoot. I wish I'd waited around to see that." Taking a black felt box out of his pocket he said, "I've been dreaming of the four of us becoming a family. Will you marry me, Jayne?"

She stared at the diamond ring for a long time. "Oh, Wes, it's beautiful." She might have wanted him to believe that she had all the haughtiness of one of his barn cats, but Wes saw the tears glazing her eyes, the tremble on her lips as she said, "It's interesting that you mentioned dreaming, because I had another interesting dream last night. I'll tell you about it later, but first I have to warn you."

"What…you have an evil twin?"

"No. Burke is my only full-fledged brother. Our parents are a piece of work, but I'm pretty sure you'll be able to handle them. But statistics show that second marriages have an even greater failure rate than first marriages."

Wes suddenly realized that he was standing in the middle of a bedroom with the woman he loved and who had just agreed to marry him. The last thing he wanted to talk about was the likelihood of divorce. But this was important to Jayne, so he would say it one time.

"*This* marriage won't fail."

"Nobody thinks their marriage will—"

"Besides," he cut in. "I would never agree to an amicable divorce the way Sherm did. I'll never agree to a divorce, period. Now what do you say? Will you marry me peacefully? Or will I have to hog-tie you and carry you kicking and screaming to the altar?"

"You're a bully, Stryker."

"I know. You've gotta love me for it, doncha?"

Jayne started out shaking her head, but wound up nodding. "Maybe I am nuts, but yes, I'd love to marry you."

He let out a yowling "Yee-ha!" and twirled her off her feet.

Feeling weightless and breathless, Jayne held on for dear life. Something told her the union would be long and true and wonderful. However, she doubted it would be peaceful. Oh, no. There would be kids fighting, wind howling, she and Wes arguing.

In a serious moment, Wes set her on her feet and stared into her eyes. Placing the ring on her finger, he said, "I'll do my best to make you happy, Jayne, to support you and the kids. Annabell's thinking about coming to Jasper Gulch until she's fully recovered. Things will be lean for the first few years. It took most of my rodeo winnings to pay the back taxes on the ranch and to make the repairs. I'm going to have to take out a mortgage to get the herd started. Once the ranch is profitable, I'll buy you anything you want.''

"Anything?'' she asked.

He nodded gravely. "Just name it.''

"I'll have to think about it and let you know. How much money do you think it'll take to get the ranch underway?''

Wes felt dizzy. Not that that was unusual when he spent a lot of time talking to Jayne. How much money did he need? He hated to scare her, but he had to be truthful about the future, so he named a figure and waited for her to react.

She didn't even flinch. She simply chewed on her lower lip for a moment, then calmly said, "It'll take me a few days to transfer the funds.''

Jayne had never seen Wes so quiet. At his dumbfounded expression, she placed a hand to his cheek and said, "I told you I was in advertising. Did I forget to mention that I owned half the company? It was one of the things Sherm and I had had to divvy up. I probably should have told you sooner, but the subject never came up, and really, I don't see—''

"I'm not taking your money. And what else have you forgotten to mention?''

"Me? You're the one who's dated every buckle bunny on the rodeo circuit. And you are so taking my money.''

"How do you know who I've dated? And I am not.''

"Logan might have mentioned something once. And yes, you are.''

"I mean it, Jayne. I'm a man, and I have a little pride.''

"I'm a woman, and I happen to be in love with you. Madly, passionately, completely in love with you.''

"You really are an exasperating, infuriating woman, do you know that? And another thing—''

"Wes, honey?''

He paused at the interruption.

"Do you think you could shut up and kiss me?''

For an instant Wes felt the way he had when his feet had slipped out from under him on Christmas morning. Weightless. Breathless. And even though he knew there was going to be hell to pay when he landed, he felt a smile coming on, and a never-ending awareness take hold deep in his body.

Jayne's breath caught in her throat at all the emotions she saw shimmer across his expression. He lowered his face by degrees, and slanted her a look that won him a quivery pout because she knew that he wouldn't let her run roughshod over him. And he knew that she knew.

"Well?" she asked, her gaze on his lower lip that was enticingly close and yet not quite close enough. "Are you going to kiss me, cowboy?"

The breath rushed out of him. The moment before his mouth covered hers, she heard him say, "Whatever you say, ma'am. Whatever you say."

* * * * *

More books in the
BACHELOR GULCH *series are on their way.*
Watch for Josie's story, coming soon from
Sandra Steffen and Silhouette Romance.

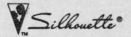

If you enjoyed what you just read,
then we've got an offer you can't resist!

Take 2 bestselling love stories FREE!

Plus get a FREE surprise gift!

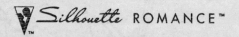

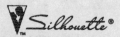

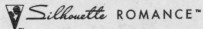

Coming in May 1999

BABY *Fever*

by
New York Times Bestselling Author

KASEY MICHAELS

When three sisters hear their biological
clocks ticking, they know it's
time for action.

But who will they get to father their babies?

**Find out how the road to motherhood
leads to love in this brand-new collection.**

Available at your favorite retail outlet.

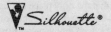

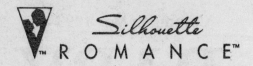

COMING NEXT MONTH